ORPHAN TRAIN ESCAPE

HEARTS ON THE RAILS

RACHEL WESSON

PROLOGUE

New York 1893, Carmel's Mission

*L*ily Doherty sang softly as she moved through the rooms of the sanctuary. It had taken the best part of five years to get Carmel's Mission, the sanctuary named after her husband's grandmother, working as she hoped. Initially, her project had been met by skepticism. So many New Yorkers believed the poor chose to live in poverty and decay. But she had persevered. With her husband,

1

Charlie, and Mr. Prentice—Mr. P as she liked to call him—behind her, she hadn't let any setback stop her from moving forward. Dr. Elmwood had also been a huge asset, helping the ladies and children with medical issues free of charge.

Finally, things began to change. Word spread among the people she most wanted to reach, that the help she offered didn't come with many conditions. She didn't require them to change religions or start attending church in order to be helped. She didn't impose her beliefs on anyone. Yes, she had Father Nelson and Pastor Adams working with her. Both men were similar and believed being a Christian meant you helped all those in need not just those you considered worthy. Of course, their hope was always that others would see their way of life as the best way and follow suit. It worked, too, as both men saw an increase in attendances at their respective services.

Many members of the local community had got behind her idea and had offered their help as well, not only in money but also in labor. They were the people who touched her heart more. The men and women who had toiled all week long but still gave the sanctuary an hour or so. The women cleaned the rooms and made the large pots of soup she distributed to those in need as well as the residents of the sanctuary. Lily hoped it would continue although the numbers requiring her help were rising. She was particularly concerned about the number of children living on the streets. Something more had to be done for them.

Charlie was worried about the economy. He had his head stuck in the New York Times again this morning. Where had the happy-go-lucky lad she had married gone? Smiling, she admitted to herself they had both grown in the last five years. Their marriage was a joy to both of them; their respective work a blessing. Charlie helped with legal issues as and when they arose. His employer, a man he had saved in the great whiteout of '88, had recognized

Charlie's strengths and his position with the firm was rock solid.

She tried to be more positive about the economy, although she had to admit it was scary hearing about the next bank closing. Mr. P also seemed more on edge than usual. And the news from her friends back in Clover Springs, Colorado was heartbreaking. Both Erin and Ellen had written about the number of miners finding their way to the town, their jobs gone overnight. The price of silver had dropped drastically and was still moving downward.

Her office door opened, admitting a matronly lady. Lily smiled at the woman who worked almost as hard as she did.

"Good morning, Lily. Lovely day isn't it?" Mrs. Wilson's smile could light up a room.

"It is indeed, Mrs. Wilson. How are the ladies?"

"Doing much better now you've secured more work for them. They were scared you would send them back onto the streets."

The news about the economy always hit the poor worst of all, as they were the ones to pay a heavier price. When you lived day to day, never having sufficient money to meet all your bills, any reduction in earnings would be devastating.

"You know I would never do that." She prayed to God she'd never have to. But if the economy did spiral downwards, would she have enough to keep the Sanctuary going?

"I know Lily, but you have to remember not all of them know you like I do. They don't know you were once as poor as they are. They wouldn't believe me if I told them about your past. You are very much a lady now."

Lily grinned as she looked at her clothes. If you judged her solely on the way she was dressed, it was obvious she was financially secure. Her dress, while modest in fashion, was made of the highest quality cotton. Her hands were lily-white and not red raw like many of the women in the soup lines. She was lucky.

She'd left a horrible past behind with the

help of Doc Erin and Mick Quinn from Clover Springs. They had brought her to New York where she met Mr. P. Their visit coincided with the biggest tragedy to hit New York. Lily shivered, remembering how many had died during the '88 blizzard. Was it really five years ago?

CHAPTER 1

*B*ridget Collins pushed the lank hair out of her eyes as she stretched her back. Everything ached from her head to her toes and it wasn't yet midday. She could only imagine how bad it was for the older women who worked here. She was supposed to be in her prime – yet at nineteen she felt every year of her age and a hundred more.

Oaks Laundry, where she worked, was situated in the basement of a tenement building where fresh air was the stuff of daydreams. She wished she could take a break but her supervisor, Mr. Webster, was even more on edge than usual. Mr. Oaks senior, the owner, must be on site. He was strict, although she preferred him to his son. The way young Mr. Oaks looked at her made her want to crawl out of her own skin.

She pushed the shirts back into the water, having scrubbed the cuffs and collars with the harsh lye soap. Her thoughts drifted back to her childhood in Ireland, like the green, open fields she had run through with her brothers and sisters on their way to school. Mam had insisted her children would do better by learning to read and write. Only a proper education gave the poor a chance in life. Poor mam. Bridget never thought she would be glad her mam was dead. But it would have killed her to see how her children were faring. Coming to America had been her mam's dream. She believed in the stories sent back to Ireland from people who had emigrated. This was supposed to be the land of opportunity. Bridget sighed, wondering how people had written home such tales of hope when the reality was so different.

Maura, her eldest sister was at home, her heart grieving for her fiancé, killed in the explosion at their work last weekend. In the space of two days, she had lost not only her job, but her hope for the future. David had idolized Maura, calling her his older woman – he'd been twenty to Maura's twenty-two. He had protected the whole family against the worst of tenement life. Bridget squeezed her eyes shut to stop a tear escaping. She could still see David now, his big blue eyes lit up from inside. He was always smiling. How come the good died young? Her brothers, Shane and Michael, were running wild. She suspected they were involved with one of the many gangs who preyed on the poor. Kathleen, her favorite sister, was slowly going blind sewing button holes. Liam, the youngest boy, was out collecting rags as he tried to provide for the family at six years of age. He was particularly close to Annie, his junior by two years, and couldn't bear to see her go hungry. What would they do?

* * *

"GOOD AFTERNOON BRIDGET, you look mighty pretty today."

Bridget stilled, her backbone going rigid at the sound of his voice. She hadn't seen him come in, so he'd caught her by surprise. Pretty? Covered in sweat with lank hair and red, raw hands? He needed his eyes tested.

"Good afternoon, sir." Her tone was as polite as she could make it without being servile. Yes, he was the son of the boss, but that didn't make him her better. Mam said the goodness of one's heart was the value of a man, not how much money he kept in the bank.

"I need to see you in the office," Mr. Oaks said. "There has been a complaint."

As soon as he walked away, confident she

would follow, she wilted. What type of complaint had there been this time? She was sick of his attempts to get her alone. How many times did she have to tell him she was a good, Catholic girl? What he wanted from her was for her husband alone. She pulled the tub away from the heat and, wiping her stinging hands on her apron, walked slowly to the office.

She could feel the eyes on her back, although anyone checking on the women would think they hadn't stopped working. The tension in the air was palpable. Those who had worked for Oaks Laundry and Sewing for years knew what being summoned to the office meant. For the men, it was bad news. For the women, the younger ones anyway, it was a lot worse. She saw a couple of the women cross themselves and hoped they had shared a prayer for her as well. She pushed her shoulders back. Whatever he threatened her with this time, she still wasn't going to give in to him. Never.

"There you are," he said as she entered his

office. "The walk across the floor seems to take you longer each time, Bridget."

She ignored the reprimand but stood with her hands balled at her sides, her fingernails hurting the insides of her palms. His grey blue eyes, almost colorless, were fixated on her chest as he addressed her. She glanced at his suit, the golden chain from his watch hanging from the pocket of his waistcoat another reminder of how wealthy he was. She glanced at his face momentarily, thinking of the comments someone from the factory floor had made about him wishing to model his appearance on the Prince of Wales. She had never seen a picture of the Prince but wondered if his wife thought a full beard and long whiskers to be attractive. It certainly didn't suit Mr. Oaks making him look even uglier than his behavior.

The office door closed behind her, shutting off most of the noise of the shop floor. The air in the office would have been sweeter than that of the laundry but for his presence. There was a pervading sense of evil about him, something she couldn't explain in words.

She refused to look him in the eye. Instead, she stared at a point above his head.

"Why don't you sit down Bridget and have some soup. It's delicious."

The smell of the soup stirred her stomach. She hoped it wouldn't start grumbling. She didn't want the man to know how hungry she was. But if he thought she was going to sell herself for some food, he was wrong. It was time to try to take a little control back. She was an employee, not his servant. Or at least it was supposed to be that way.

"You mentioned a complaint, sir."

"Yes, but not against you, Bridget. Your work is always to the highest standard."

What was she doing in his office then? He hadn't said her work was of high quality when she got demoted from the sewing department to the laundry. But she kept her mouth shut and waited. He had something on his mind; she could tell by the tone of his voice. He was baiting her. To him, she wasn't a person, but a plaything. Something to amuse himself with when he got bored. And she wasn't the first.

When she started in the laundry, the girl called to the office on several occasions was Mary Rourke. Mary, who ended up in the Hudson River, her swelling abdomen evidence of her so-called crime. Poor Mary. She'd been desperate. This evil man had told her she had to pay for her father's mistakes. The same father who had thrown his own daughter out when the evidence of what she had done came to light.

But Bridget wasn't Mary.

"You aren't curious about why you are in here?" he asked.

"I expect you will tell me, sir."

She had to be careful. Her temper was rising, and it could easily cost Bridget her job. Her pay wasn't much, but it was enough to keep the roof over their heads when combined with what Kathleen earned. They depended on what young Liam earned from rag picking to supplement the cost of food.

"A girl in the sewing section…"

Her heart thumped when he didn't complete his sentence. She could feel his eyes boring into her body. She knew he was talking about Kathleen, but she was a good girl. She wouldn't give cause for complaint unless someone had done something to her.

"If you have touched her, you—" she spat.

"Bridget Collins, remember yourself. You know I wouldn't put a finger on such an insipid creature. I prefer my women to have fire in their bellies. Makes for a much more satisfying arrangement if you catch my drift."

He wasn't exactly subtle. Of course, she understood him.

"But as the complaint was made, we had no choice but to send your sister home. Her position has already been filled."

Her stomach dropped at the same time as her heart started beating faster. He'd fired Kathleen. Now, at a time when jobs were like gold dust.

Her family couldn't survive without Kathleen's wages. But then he would know that. He was using the situation to remind her he held complete power over her future and that of her siblings. Her fingernails dug deeper into her palms.

"Don't you have something to say?" he asked.

"No, sir." She wasn't going to apologize. Kathleen hadn't done anything wrong, she was sure of it. The sixteen-year-old girl was too shy and afraid of her own shadow to cause trouble. Mam used to say Kathleen was born with a heart too sensitive for this world.

He moved closer to her, blocking her exit. She stepped away from him until the office table prevented her escape.

He pushed a strand of hair away from her face while she held her body rigid, so it wouldn't flinch. She wasn't going to show him any fear. He delighted in making people fear him.

"Now, tell me Bridget, how will we make

this situation work? I have been told to fire you as well. We have to make an example, to show the other workers that laziness and poor workmanship will not be tolerated."

She stared over his shoulder, refusing to rise to his tricks. They both knew there wasn't a lazy bone in her sister's body. But protesting that wouldn't change anything.

He moved so close it was almost as if the only thing separating them were their clothes. She could feel his breath on her neck, his expensive cologne making her nostrils sting.

"Bridget, we could have so much fun together. You wouldn't go hungry. You might be able to afford a nicer home. Your brothers wouldn't be in danger of being locked up."

She couldn't help flinching. What did he know of Michael and Shane?

"Yes, I know your brothers. In fact, I may have mentioned my concerns to a couple of friends on the force. They can't be allowed to prey on the poor. Making people's lives miserable with their thieving, drinking, and debauchery."

If she had been anywhere else, she may have been amused by the irony of this man using those terms about someone else. Isn't that what he did every day? He may not steal in the conventional sense, but keeping his workers locked in this basement for twelve hours a day and paying them a pitiful wage was a different form of stealing, wasn't it?

"You will have to be very nice to me, Bridget. I hold the power to destroy your little family. Although it would pain me, believe me, I will do it."

"Pain you? Nothing could make you feel anything with a heart of iron. You won't get anything from me, Stephen Oaks. I told you before, and I will tell you again. My body isn't for sale, not at any price."

He grinned, making her stomach roil. "Now we both know that isn't true. Every woman has her price. For women of my class, it's marriage and a suitable home. In return, they know they have to fulfil their duty. For women of your class, some good food usually is enough for them to—"

"Not me. I was brought up better than that. Now do your worst, but you won't have me."

He trailed his lips along her neck, leaving her skin wet as he gripped her arms savagely.

"Believe me I will. I always get what I want."

DESPERATE, Bridget's hands flew behind her. There must be something on the desk she could use to defend herself. His grip on her tightened as his lips moved all over her face. She refused to let him kiss her, causing him to call her a horrible word. He pushed himself against her. Time was running out. Her fingers grabbed wildly on the desk, finally finding something sharp. A letter opener. She grabbed it without thinking and slashed at him. The element of surprise was on her side. Her aim was off, but she still managed to slice his ear. His blood dripped over her hand just as he cried out and moved slightly away, his focus on his injury. She pushed him farther and ran to the door. Opening it, she flew from the office and didn't stop until she was halfway home. What had she done? He was bound to report her and then what would happen to her family? She picked up her skirts and fled home, back to the tenement building.

CHAPTER 2

"Bridget, what happened? Kathleen came home and went to bed without a word," Bridget's eldest sister, Maura, said.

Bridget didn't stop as she stepped inside their room in the tenement. She didn't even close the door behind her in her usual attempt to block out the disgusting stench.

"Maura, pack up everything," she said, fighting to remain calm. "We have to get out of here now."

"But why? Where will we go?" Maura whined.

"I don't know, but the police will be here soon. They will put the children in the asylum and…. Oh Maura, I'll tell you later but please get ready. We don't have much time." Bridget saw Kathleen get out of bed and dress quickly. She sent her white-faced sister out to find Liam and Annie.

"Where will we go?" Maura repeated, standing still as if they had all the time in the world. "This is our home."

Bridget glanced around the windowless room that had sheltered them for the last three years ever since daddy had lost his job on the railways. Kathleen had covered the biggest cracks with newspaper in an effort to make the hovel homelier. The newspapers didn't keep out any of the sounds around them. The rat's claws scraping against the plaster, their high-pitched squeaks as they fought each other for dominance. She didn't know which was worse, the noise of the rats, the drunken neighbors singing bawdy sounds, or the noisy love-making that seemed to follow.

It was impossible to know how many people lived in these tenements. The multistory brick building had been built years before for far grander purposes and certainly wasn't designed to hold so many immigrants. Now, each room was tenanted, sometimes by more than one family. Bridget knew they had been lucky not being forced to share their room with strangers.

Lucky? If daddy hadn't fallen foul of the landlord, wrongly accused of a crime, their lives would have been so much better in Ireland. They had been poor but happy. The air had been fresh and there was more room to move around. If she closed her eyes, she could see her mam spinning wool in the evening, exchanging a warm smile with their daddy sitting by the fire. Bridget's mam had been a powerhouse of energy, by day working as a seamstress in the big house, and in her spare time, she had raised chickens, selling the eggs at the local store. Sometimes she sold cheese and brown bread at the market. Now Mam and

Daddy were dead and all they had left was each other.

Bridget reined in her impatience with her sister. Maura was the eldest, but she was behaving worse than Annie, her four-year-old sister.

Thankfully, Bridget had thought about where they should go on her run back home. They would go to Father Nelson at the church. He would help them. He had to. He'd believe she was only protecting herself, wouldn't he? He wasn't like the previous priest. He was different. She had to take a chance on him. It was their only option. They certainly couldn't stay here, just waiting to be picked up.

"Where are Michael and Shane?" she asked her sister.

"Out, as always." Maura's resigned reply spoke volumes as she poked at the fire. Maura had started dinner, lighting a small fire on the paving stones in the corner of the room. The smoke made everyone's eyes water, but it was the only way to cook the potatoes which were baking in the embers. Maura had done all the cooking since David had died. It was all she did. The boys ran wild but, in fairness, even David hadn't managed to control the boys. They were old enough to fend for themselves, being fifteen and seventeen.

"We can't wait for them. I'll send Colm Fleming to find them and tell them not to come back here but to head straight for the church. Mrs. Fleming may use the room—we've paid for the next two weeks." Bridget looked around the small room they used as a bedroom, kitchen, and everything else. If only she hadn't met the rent collector last evening. She would have that money to tide them over. But she couldn't live by "if only." It raised more questions than it answered.

"Oh Bridget, I can't believe this. David was so sure things were turning around for us and now it's all gone wrong. I just can't do it, I can't…"

Bridget watched in horror as her elder sister descended into a fit of screaming.

She slapped Maura hard on the face. "Pull yourself together. You are the eldest, not me. Mam depended on us to protect the young ones."

Maura stared at her resentfully, but she didn't say a word. Instead she took the potatoes out of the fire and threw clay on the embers to put it out.

Bridget packed up their pitiful belongings and, within fifteen minutes of Bridget coming home, the room was empty. Kathleen came back with the younger children, all remained tight-lipped as they looked from Bridget and Maura to the bags at their feet.

"We have to go see Father Nelson about a new home. It's time for a change," Bridget said, trying to inject some enthusiasm into her voice. She didn't want to scare the young 'uns.

"I like it here. Mrs. Fleming is nice to us. Why do we have to leave?" Liam asked, his hand in Annie's. The little girl sucked her other thumb, her eyes wide with fear. Bridget's heart clenched with hate for Mr. Oaks and his like. This was the only home the children remembered and now they were losing that too.

"Don't worry Liam. The next house will be nicer. I promise." She crossed her fingers hoping she would be proved right. Looking over the child's head at the dirty, damp walls, it wouldn't take much to find somewhere nicer to live.

Mrs. Fleming wished them well, hugging all of them as she dabbed at her eyes with her apron. "Don't you worry about nothing, darlings. I will tell them fellas you went to family in Jersey. By the time they chase after that goose, you will have flown. May God have mercy on their souls as straight to the devil they will go for preying on such lovely girls as youse. Thank God your poor mam is dead and buried."

THEY TRUDGED THROUGH THE STREETS. Nobody commented on their sorry little procession, too wrapped up in their own survival.

Father Nelson was in the church when they arrived. Bridget told him the full story of what had happened, watching his facial expressions closely. At one point he looked so furious she took a step back from him.

"Bridget Collins," he said. "Never be afraid of standing up for yourself. You are not to blame. If I wasn't a man of God, I would… well, the least said about that the better. Let's go and see what my lovely housekeeper can rustle up for you. A full belly will make you all feel better."

"Father, what if the police come here?"

"You let me worry about that, young Bridget. I have some very good friends on the force myself. The man you are running from isn't the only one with connections. Come on, child, take that look off your face. You are all safe here."

Bridget wanted to believe him, but she

couldn't. She knew how it worked. The rich always won.

But her younger siblings didn't need to know how she felt. She forced a smile on her face and gathered them together as they followed the priest into his house. His housekeeper's reception wasn't as warm. She stared at them. Looking through her eyes, Bridget could see the reason for her distaste. They were all filthy, and the younger one's heads were crawling. But what could they do? There was no running water in the hovel they called home, never mind soap. Bridget pushed her hair back. They had done their best.

"Mrs. Riordan, these poor children are running from evil. They need our help. A decent meal followed by a hot bath and a good scrub is what's in order. You provide the meal and we will look after everything else later."

"Yes, Father Nelson."

"Now, I need to go out. I shall return shortly. Bridget, could you come with me please?"

Torn between wanting to stay with her siblings and doing what the priest asked, Bridget hesitated. Maura wasn't being particularly helpful, but even she wouldn't let any harm come to the children. Would she? Father Nelson misinterpreted her reluctance to go with him. He assumed she was hungry.

"Have some food first and then we will go together. Your family will be safe here. Mrs. Riordan may not smile much but sure the woman has a heart of gold," Father Nelson whispered. Bridget looked at the housekeeper and hoped he was right.

Maybe the lady was someone who found it hard to show her feelings.

CHAPTER 3

*L*ily had just finished her dinner when she heard a knock on the door.

"Mrs. Doherty. Father Nelson and a young woman are here to see you," Peters, her butler, informed her.

"Send them in, Peters, and ask Cook to make some tea. You know how Father Nelson likes her baking."

"Yes Ma'am."

Lily smiled at Peters. Despite the fact that he knew her story, he insisted on treating her like gentry. He'd told her she was the reason he was still alive. When they had first met, during the aftermath of the blizzard, he had nothing to live for. His family were long gone, and he'd lost his job. She'd offered him a position as soon as he recovered his health. His friend, Mary, was taken on as the cook. Both lived in the servant's quarters and worked their hardest to keep Lily and her husband comfortable. They were so loyal, you would often find both of them lending a hand at the sanctuary on their days off. Peter helped to amuse the children while Mary helped Cook prepare meals for the people sheltering there.

"Father Nelson, how nice to see you," Lily greeted. "But on such a terrible night. You're both soaked through. Come in and warm yourselves by the fire. Peters has gone for some tea and some of Cook's baking."

"Words to warm the cockles of my heart, Lily darling," Father Nelson said, beaming. "This lovely young woman is a friend of mine. Bridget Collins meet Lily Doherty."

Lily shook Bridget's hand, but what she really wanted to do was give the poor girl a hug and wipe the desperation and fear from her eyes.

"Come in please. I'm afraid Charlie has to work this evening, but he may come down later. They have a rather big case on their hands."

"Charlie is Lily's lovely husband. He works for Harrington Law & Investigative Services," Father Nelson explained to Bridget.

Lily glanced at Bridget again. The poor girl looked as if she would fall over.

"Can I offer you something more substantial than tea? Cook made some wonderful soup earlier."

"No thank you, Lily. We ate before we came out," Father Nelson explained. "Bridget, you can trust Lily one hundred percent. She will help you. I promise that."

"In any way I can, Bridget," Lily confirmed.

"Bridget had a very unpleasant experience today. It seems the son of her boss tried to take advantage of her. It wasn't the first time, but today he pushed her too far. In self-defense, she struck him with a letter opener. He may have been injured as she thinks she drew blood. He had already fired her sister and threatened her brothers with the law. Wisely, she gathered up her younger siblings and brought them to the church."

"Oh, your poor girl. What an ordeal. Who did you work for?"

"Mr. Oaks, ma'am," Bridget answered.

"Call me Lily, please. I have heard of Mr. Oaks. He is known for being a hard taskmaster, but I never heard rumors of him chasing his staff."

"It's the son ma'am—I mean, Lily. He tried this before, not just with me. My friend, well, she was a good bit older than me. Used to look after us kids when we were younger, and Mam was working. Her name was Mary Rourke."

Lily looked to the priest as the name rang bells.

"Yes, it's the girl we found in the Hudson

shortly after I moved to this Parish. She was in the family way. Her parents put her out on the street. Father Donnelly condemned her. The poor child believed she had no alternative."

Lily tried to stamp on the revulsion and anger she felt toward Father Donnelly, the Priest who had used his position to abuse the poor he was supposed to look after. It would do Bridget no good at all to discuss that sad time. She took Bridget's hands in hers and could feel her shaking.

"Listen to me Bridget. You are safe, and nobody is going to hurt you. We will help. Tell me about your family."

"I have three brothers and three sisters, well that's what's left of us. Maura is twenty two, I am nineteen, Michael is seventeen, Kathleen's sixteen and Shane is fifteen. The two youngest are six and four, Liam and Annie. Michael and Shane are almost grown men, and have fallen in with a bad crowd, but they are old enough to fend for themselves. I have tried speaking to them but it's hard to argue for goodness if it brings hunger when the bad ways of the gangs give them a chance."

Lily listened, her heart aching for the boys even as Bridget described them. They had little choice, really. At their age, without jobs, it was only a matter of time before the gangs would get a hold of them.

"Da died in an accident on the tracks three years ago. Mam died soon after, the loss of da and the baby was too much for her."

"Oh Bridget, I am so sorry."

"It's the little ones I worry for most. Annie is only four and Liam, God love him, acts like a man, but he's only six. I fear if they stay in New York, they will end up in the asylum or worse. Maura, my eldest sister, lost both her fiancé and her job in the explosion at Wentworth's iron forge last week and my sister Kathleen and I both worked for Mr. Oaks. We have nowhere to turn."

"You have us Bridget. You and your sisters can work for me at the Sanctuary. We have positions for skilled seamstresses. Maura can look after the younger children along with some other orphans currently lodging at the sanctuary. We usually don't have children living there but these are unusual times." Lily didn't explain what she meant by that statement. She wasn't about to mention they were gathering some children to send on the orphan train. That would only scare Bridget. "Father Nelson may be able to reach out to your brothers. You can live at the sanctuary for now. I am sure Mrs. Riordan will be relieved to hear that." Lily could only imagine what the priest's housekeeper was making of the situation. She was the least likely person who should be employed by Father Nelson, but maybe it was her unpleasant nature that kept her in the position. Father Nelson would be inundated with requests for help otherwise. Like Lily, he was only able to do so much, and the needs of the community were overpowering. She couldn't help everyone, but she was definitely going to help this poor young woman. Mr. Oaks junior had met his match.

CHAPTER 4

*B*ridget looked at the woman wondering if she were some sort of angel. She had just offered Bridget a job as well as a home within five minutes of meeting her. She pinched her arm, but she didn't wake up.

"Ah, here is Peters with the tea," Lily said. "Why don't you make yourselves comfortable? I will send the carriage around to Mrs. Riordan to collect your family."

Bridget sat on the very edge of the sofa, worried she would dirty it. She couldn't help but admire her surroundings. It was evident Lily was comfortable. The walls were papered, not painted, and the tea service appeared to be real china. Just like Lady Danbury's set. Her mind flew back to Galway when Maura had taken her up to see their Mam who worked as a seamstress in the big house. The cook had given them some biscuits and a glass of milk each. A maid had been washing up the china when they called and had let Bridget hold one cup. She blinked away the memories. She had to focus on the future now.

"Thank you, ma'am—I mean, Lily."

"Now Bridget, you can relax and taste some of Cook's fine cakes. They will melt on your tongue. Mary is the finest cook this side of the Hudson." Father Nelson almost licked his lips.

"Father Nelson is easy to please," Lily said. "Bake him a cake and he will do anything for you."

Bridget's mouth fell open as Lily teased the

priest, but he didn't take offense. Instead, he laughed along.

"So, from what you said, Maura is in mourning. Is she capable of helping to look after the younger children do you think?" Lily asked.

Was she? Lily had no idea, but she wasn't about to admit it. In her world, people didn't have time to stop and mourn a death. She nodded. Maura would help, if she didn't Bridget would kill her, but talking about killing her sister was probably not wise given the circumstances.

"She isn't much of a seamstress," Bridget said. "She did the office work in the iron works. Mam insisted on Maura staying at school as long as she could. She is good with her writing and her math."

"Oh, how interesting. Usually the women we see are brought up to get married and have families," Lily commented.

"Yes, Mam was determined education was a key to a better future. I am glad she isn't here to see what a mess we have made of things," Bridget said.

"Stop that now. There is no sense in blaming yourself. You can't help the way things turned out no more than you can help the evil urges Master Oaks suffers from. Now finish your tea."

"Yes ma'am—I mean, Lily."

CHAPTER 5

The cab stopped at the Sanctuary which was situated on a quiet, clean road. There were no rubbish tips teaming with rats and other vermin, no street vendors or teams of people milling around. It was a two-story brick house. They climbed the steps to the front door, Lily taking a key from her purse, and opening the lock, stepping back to let the little family enter before her. The smell of lavender and lemon pervaded the premises, every surface gleaming, even the wooden floor with its highly polished shine.

First, Lily showed them where they would sleep. Bridget looked around the room with the two beds, both covered in colorful quilts. Being tall, she had to stoop to avoid the pitch of the ceiling at the edges but that was no discomfort. The center of the room allowed her to stand straight. It might be the attic, but it was a palace compared to what they were used to.

"Real beds, Bridget," Maura said, gazing at them in awe. "Do you believe it?"

"Maura, I think I could believe anything after tonight."

Lily showed them to the indoor bathroom, a true luxury. The children were each given a hot bath first and their clothes were taken away to be burnt. The rags they wore were crawling with vermin. Annie had cried when Lily took her favorite rag doll away, but she soon cheered up when Lily promised to replace it with a new doll the following morning. Then it was the older girls' turns. Bridget couldn't believe how much better she felt after washing the grime out of her hair.

When she was finished, she saw Lily had left her some new clothes as well. The dresses, although secondhand, were of much better quality than those she had been wearing.

"Look, Bridget, that pink shirtwaist would suit you."

"I took that for myself, Kathleen."

"Maura, it doesn't go with your coloring at all, it will look much better on Bridget."

Shocked by her sister's uncharacteristic outburst, Bridget pulled Kathleen into her arms. The younger girl's shoulders shook as she sobbed. "It's all my fault. If I hadn't lost my job, we wouldn't have to stay here."

"Kathleen Collins, you dry your eyes this minute. Haven't we landed on our feet? It's thanking Mr. Oaks we should be doing. I've never felt so clean in all my life. Maura, you can have the dress if you prefer it."

"No, Bridget, Kathleen is right. It would suit you much better. I will take this one." Maura pointed to a light green dress. "The blue one will suit Kathleen, it matches her eyes."

Bridget gave Maura a thankful look as Kathleen's sobs slowly subsided.

"Can we stay here forever?" Annie asked, tugging at Lily's skirt.

"I don't know darling. Now, why don't you cuddle up with Liam and go to sleep? It's been a long day," Bridget answered as she kissed her sister.

"I think this is what Heaven looks like," Annie sighed.

Bridget didn't respond to the young girl's comment. Instead, she prayed with them and then tucked them into the larger bed. Maura would share with them and she and Kathleen would share the smaller bed. Lily had offered them a room of their own, but Bridget declined, knowing her family would prefer to be together.

"Bridget, do you think I will be good enough to work for Miss Lily?" Kathleen asked.

"Of course you will," Bridget said. "There was nothing wrong with you, or your work. Mr. Oaks fired you out of spite."

"Lily is so lovely, isn't she? She's beautiful and kind. I'm so glad we met her," Kathleen said, her eyes already closing.

You and me both, thought Bridget. But she didn't say anything out loud.

Despite feeling warm, full, and clean for the first time in a very long time, Bridget couldn't sleep. She sensed Oaks wouldn't be so easily put off. Lily had said she was safe here but how did she know? Her eyes finally closed as she fell into an exhausted sleep, but her dreams became nightmares. In each one she was running and running only to end up in Mr. Oaks' clutches.

CHAPTER 6

 ridget and Kathleen left Maura with the younger children the next morning and headed downstairs to the sewing room, following the direction of the cook.

"Good morning, ladies. Welcome to our workshop. My name is Mrs. Wilson and I am in charge. Kathleen, I have been told you have experience in button holes."

"Yes, Mrs. Wilson. I've worked at a number of tasks, the last one being the button holes."

"Good, and you Bridget?" Mrs. Wilson asked.

"I've done more or less the same as Kathleen, only my stitching isn't as neat as hers," Bridget said. "Lately I've been working in the laundry." She didn't add that Mr. Oaks Junior had sent her there to see if he could break her spirit. She should have started looking for a new job as soon as that happened but there had been so little time.

"Have either of you used a sewing machine like this one before?"

Bridget couldn't believe her eyes. The machine was one of the modern ones. She touched it gently.

"No, Mrs. Wilson, but we are both quick learners. Aren't we Kathleen?"

"Yes ma'am," her sister agreed.

"Good. Sarah will show you both how to use it, but first let me introduce you to all the women here. Most have been with us for some time now, but they know what it was like when they first came. We believe in helping each other out. We get paid for what we turn in as a group, not for individual work."

Bridget didn't know how to respond to that, so she kept quiet. Would they hold the group back as they had yet to learn how to use the machines?

"Bella and Jess have each volunteered to sit with you so that you have an experienced seamstress to ask questions of," Mrs. Wilson explained. "That will happen after Sarah gives you some lessons. Do you have any questions?"

"No ma'am but thank you. We won't let you down," Bridget said.

"I know that. Lily is an excellent judge of character. Oh, here is Sarah now. I will leave you to it and check on you later."

"Thank you," Bridget answered for both of them as Kathleen appeared to have lost the use of her voice.

Sarah turned out to be a very pleasant lady whose idea of working hard included making the odd joke. She spoke very quickly as she worked. Bridget found it harder to get used to the new machine than Kathleen did. After a couple of hours, it was as though Kathleen had been using the machine for years.

"You have a natural talent, Kathleen. I'm excited at the quality of the work you will produce," Sarah said. "Bella will take care of you from now on. You are ready to move to her side."

Bridget waited to hear if she would be moving to work with Jess, but instead Sarah handed her some more pieces of material.

"You need a little more practice, but I am sure you will get the hang of it. Eventually." Sarah smiled, making Bridget feel a little better.

She wasn't about to tell the girl their mother had been a seamstress to a real lady back in Ireland. Her mam would turn in her grave if she saw the mess Bridget was making of what Sarah called the easy stitches.

AT NOON EVERYONE stopped working when a bell sounded. The women pushed back from their work benches to stretch their arms and legs.

Bridget looked up in alarm.

"Don't look so frightened, the bell means it's time for lunch. Lily insists we stop to eat. It's not like the other places you've worked in, is it?" Sarah asked.

Bridget shook her head. For one, all the staff were women and treated each other with respect. There were bound to be disagreements, particularly in a group of women, some of which had been settled quietly that morning. If that was the case all the time, she could see why the women looked happier than the usual factory workforce. Tantalizing smells made their way into the room as the outer doors opened.

"Vegetable soup again by the smell of it," one of the girls said, sounding disappointed. "I wish she would change up the menu a little."

"Quit your moaning Maggie," said another. "It's better than bread and water."

"Maybe a diet of bread and water would do you good for a while, Sheila. Those pounds are piling on like nobody's business," the lady called Maggie retorted.

"More for that man of mine to put his arms around, ain't it?" Sheila replied.

Bridget listened to the ladies chatting. They were teasing each other, but it was friendly banter. Kathleen stepped over to her side.

"How did you go?" her sister asked. "Are you still practicing?"

"Yes, Miss I can sew anything." Bridget smiled to show Kathleen she was teasing. "I'm not as good as you are."

"You are too, Bridget, only you don't have the same patience. That's all. If you stop thinking about everything but the seam, you'll be fine."

As if it were that easy. The sanctuary was wonderful, but Bridget had seen there were few children around. She didn't think Lily's solution for them would be a long-term thing. Where would they all go? Would they stay together? What was going to happen with Maura?

"I'd best go find Maura and check she's okay," Bridget said.

"Lily left a message to say she was fine, and you were not to skip lunch," Mrs. Wilson said, walking up behind them. Bridget couldn't help feeling a little guilty, as if caught playing hooky.

"Sorry, Mrs. Wilson, I was just worried."

"I know that, Bridget, but you need to let Maura get on with things. We've all got our crosses to bear. I hope you don't think I'm being uncharitable, but from where I'm standing you need to let you sister shoulder some of your responsibilities."

Bridget didn't get much chance to ponder Mrs. Wilson's comments, as Kathleen grabbed her arm.

"See, Bridget, you got to let Maura look after the children. If you don't, you'll end up having to do it yourself. Now come on, let's get some soup. I'm starving."

Bridget let Kathleen drag her off to get the soup. She had to trust Maura, but why did the voice in her head say that was a mistake?

THE DAYS PASSED QUICKLY, and the sisters fell into a routine. Maura refused to come out of the room they shared, so she looked after the little ones while Bridget and Kathleen worked in the sewing room. Bridget gradually became quite a proficient seamstress and Mrs. Wilson praised them both for their hard work. At first, Bridget was worried this would cause an issue with the other women, but they seemed to accept them. Well, apart from one girl who kept mainly to herself.

Bridget found herself wondering about her brothers, Michael and Shane. They may have grown a bit wild, but they were still her kin. If she found them, would Lily and Father Nelson be able to help them?

"Are you away with the fairies, Bridget?" Mrs. Wilson asked as she stopped at Bridget's table to collect her work.

"Sorry Mrs. Wilson, I was thinking of my brothers," Bridget said.

"Do you want to pop upstairs to check on them?"

"Oh no, not Liam. We have two other brothers, Michael and Shane. I was just wondering how they were faring."

"They say no news is good news, but that's not much comfort," Mrs. Wilson said. "Why not speak to Lily? She may be able to find out more about them. She has a lot of contacts."

Bridget turned her attention back to her sewing. Later that afternoon, Lily came to see her.

"Bridget, would you like to accompany me on my visit later? I usually go out one evening a week to visit some friends who, for their own reasons, won't come to the sanctuary. I thought you might look for your brothers."

Bridget sent Mrs. Wilson a grateful look before turning back to Lily. "Thank you. I would love to."

"Great. Dress warmly as despite being almost summer there is a bite in the wind this evening. We will leave about six."

Bridget would borrow Maura's cloak. It was thicker than hers. She didn't want to think about Maura, who was sulking away in their little room, refusing to come out. Bridget knew she was mourning David, but surely, she had to see how desperate their situation was. Lily couldn't provide for them forever. They needed Maura to work so between the three of them they could save enough to survive on their own. Otherwise, there was no way Liam and Annie would remain with them. They would be taken away by the authorities. Bridget shivered. That was the last thing she wanted to happen.

CHAPTER 7

Six o'clock came quickly. Dressed in Maura's cloak, Bridget stood waiting at the door of the sanctuary.

"Evening, miss."

Bridget nearly fainted at the size of the man who addressed her. He was as tall as he was broad and, despite the fact that she was quite tall for a woman, he made her feel like a dwarf.

"I don't have anything," she said, trying to steady her voice.

"Tommy doesn't want anything from you,

Bridget," Lily said as she approached them. "He comes with us to protect us."

"Sorry Lily, I didn't see you there." Tommy grinned as he moved to let Lily pass. Even though he was smiling, his face was enough to scare off any trouble makers Bridget could imagine. She wondered how he had come about the hideous scar covering most of his cheek.

"Tommy is an old friend. He refuses to let me out at night alone and insists on bringing Mini Mike with him."

"That's right, miss," Tommy said. "No harm can come to Lily with me and Mini beside her."

Bridget looked around her for the other man, but he was nowhere to be seen.

"We will walk, and the boys will follow. Mike just went in to see Cook. He has a sweet tooth and she always keeps a couple of cookies for him," Lily explained.

"He never shares, so if you want some you best go get your own," Tommy added.

"Thank you, Tommy, but I'm fine." Bridget could see his eyes were lit up with kindness. Why hadn't she noticed that before? "Where are we going?"

"I thought we might go down to your old house. Maybe your old neighbors have seen your brothers. Tommy and Mike don't know them, but they have put the word out and I want to see them," Lily answered.

"Not sure my brothers will come to see you, Miss Lily."

"They'll come if they know what's good for them," Tommy growled. "Not many want to go up against us. We love Lily and we want her kept happy."

Bridget shrank back from the look on Tommy's face, but Lily squeezed her arm to reassure her.

"Tommy is quite protective of me. But don't worry, your brothers won't come to any harm. Not from my friends." Lily beamed as the door opened and a man even bigger than Tommy appeared. "You ready, Mike?"

"Yes, Lily. Cook made oatmeal cookies this time. She still won't marry me though. Can you put in a good word for me?"

Bridget could only stare at the giant of a man who laughed along with Lily. Cook was forty years old, if not older, and was about four foot nothing in her shoes. This man could almost hold her in one hand.

"Mike has been telling Cook he will marry her for years. She knows he's joking," Lily explained to Bridget.

"Am not," Mike argued. "She'd make a fine wife, although I might not keep my slim figure."

The three friends laughed while Bridget just stood there. The genuine affection between the three of them was palpable, but you would find it hard to put a less likely group together. Miss Lily looked like an angel between two giants.

"Now you can see why we are safe walking the streets. Not many would approach Mini Mike and Tommy. At least no one in their right mind."

"How did you all meet?" Bridget asked.

Lily's smile dropped at the question and Bridget wished she hadn't asked.

"That's a story for another day," Lily said. "Come on, let's get moving or it will be bedtime before we get back again."

Bridget walked alongside Lily with Tommy in front of them and Mini Mike bringing up the rear. She was amazed how many people stopped to say hello to Lily. She seemed to know everyone.

Bridget's heart started racing as they got nearer to her old home. Had Oaks come looking for her? Were her brothers still alive? Did Mrs. Fleming have anything to tell them?

She put her hand over her nose as the smell worsened, batting away some flies who buzzed annoyingly around her face. She tried to step over the worst of the foul smelling garbage scattered across the street. Little kids, barefoot and only partially dressed, ran around them not caring where their feet landed. They were covered in muck and stank to high heaven. Funny how she had lived among the stench and noise only two weeks ago. Tonight, she felt as if her stomach would revolt. She noticed Lily covering her nose occasionally. Her new friend looked up to catch Bridget watching her.

"Lavender drops. Mrs. Wilson scents my gloves to help me cope with the stench," Lily told her.

Bridget just nodded, her eyes darting everywhere as she recognized some faces. They stared at her as if she were a mirage. She smiled back but they didn't return her smiles. It was almost as if they didn't recognize her. She led the group into one of the tenements until she found their old neighbor.

"Mrs. Fleming, how are you?" Bridget asked. "How's the baby?"

"Mother of God, is it yourself, Bridget?" the woman asked, looking surprised.

"Who else would I be?" Bridget asked with a nervous laugh.

"You look lovely lass. All done up like

that. I always knew you were a beauty just like your mam. If she could see you now."

If Mam were still alive, she wouldn't look like this, Bridget thought, but kept her comments to herself.

"Excuse me Mrs. Fleming. My name is—"

"Lily Doherty," Mrs. Fleming said. "I heard of you, ma'am. You're just about as famous as the president around these parts. May God bless you and your family."

"Thank you, Mrs. Fleming," Lily said, her cheeks flushing. "I do what I can."

"You do more than that and we all know it. It's said you don't turn away anyone from your door. Is it with Miss Lily you be staying, Bridget? Actually, don't answer that. The walls have ears around this sorry place." Mrs. Fleming looked from side to side. "Will you come inside and share some tea?"

"We couldn't do that," Bridget replied, eager not to put Mrs. Fleming under pressure. She knew how little the lady had. But Lily's response amazed her.

"That would be lovely, Mrs. Fleming. Tommy and Mike have a bit of business farther up the street so if we could come inside, that would help us out."

"My door is always open to young Bridget and her family." Mrs. Fleming beamed. "Come inside. Don't mind the mess."

Bridget followed Lily inside the small room. She watched Lily's face for her reaction to the hovel, but you would think Lily had walked into a hotel. She sat without cleaning off the seat and produced a parcel from her basket.

"Some cookies with the tea," Lily explained as she offered them to Mrs. Fleming. "I don't know about you, Mrs. Fleming, but I have an awful sweet tooth. Can't drink a drop without having something to crunch on."

Bridget couldn't believe it. Lily had just offered Mrs. Fleming charity but in a way that it would be impossible for Mrs. Fleming to refuse it without being rude. She glanced at her old neighbor's face to check for any upset and instead found the woman smiling.

"Kind heart you have, Miss Lily. I'm not one for cookies, but the children will love them. Thank you kindly. Now, before we have our tea, I have some news for you, Bridget, and it's not good."

CHAPTER 8

*B*ridget's heart beat so loudly she nearly put her hands over her own ears.

"That devil Oaks has been around a couple of times," Mrs. Fleming said. "He has people watching out for your return. No doubt word of your visit will reach him soon enough."

"Oh, Mrs. Fleming, have I put you in danger?"

"Never, Bridget. You don't worry about me, that little rat knows better than to touch me. My boys would have him for dinner and then some. But you best stay away. Never come here alone, not without Mike and Tommy to keep you safe."

"What of her brothers, Mrs. Fleming? Have you seen Michael and Shane?" Lily asked.

Bridget knew by the way her old friend turned to concentrate on the tea that the news wasn't good.

"Tell me," Bridget said. "Please."

"They got taken a couple of days after you went away," Mrs. Fleming said. "Word has it they're sitting in The Tombs."

"On what charge?" Lily asked.

"You name it. Assault, theft, and God knows what else."

Bridget squeezed her eyes shut. She knew they had done some bad things, but they were still her brothers. Lily took her hand in hers.

"That is good news, Bridget," Lily comforted her.

"How?"

"We know where they are. Pascal Griffin, a policeman, is a good friend of mine. My husband works for a lawyer. Between Charlie and Pascal, we may be able to do something for them. Thank you very much, Mrs. Fleming."

"Don't thank me," Mrs. Fleming said. "I bet you my last cent that Oaks was behind it. Nobody ever touched those lads before. Begging your pardon and all, Miss Lily, but what they were doing wasn't new around here. It wasn't like what that devil Oaks has been doing to the women under his father's employment for years. Nobody's going to put him in the Tombs though, are they?"

"No, probably not," Lily said. "But then we can't change the world, Mrs. Fleming. All we can do is try our best to change one person at a time. Speaking of which, I was wondering if you knew of anyone who might need our help?"

Bridget couldn't believe her ears. Everyone around these parts could do with better food, jobs, housing. But Lily was asking for actual examples.

"Aye, there are a few," Mrs. Fleming said.

"At that house of pleasure down by Five Points. A couple of young girls turned up there a week or so ago. Real young, Miss Lily. It's not right what that group are doing."

"Agreed," Lily said. "But there is little I can do about them at the moment, aside from provide the police with information. What about families close to you?"

"I'm not sure my neighbors would like me telling their secrets. Begging your pardon, not that I am trying to stop you helping them only…well people got their pride," Mrs. Fleming said.

"True, and that is how it should be," Lily answered. Then, as if it hadn't been her plan all along, Lily suggested, "What about if I got Tommy and Mike to drop off some food and clothes here with you Mrs. Fleming? Then you could give it out to whomever you deem fit."

"You do that?" Bridget couldn't stop herself from asking.

"Yes Bridget, we do. It's too little for so many, but maybe it can help someone from ending up in the Tombs or worse. All we ask is that the people we help, help someone else along the way. Not now, but in the future when their circumstances improve."

Bridget could only stare at Lily. She wished she had known of the lady before the incident with Mr. Oaks but wishing wasn't going to change anything.

"I can do that, Miss Lily," Mrs. Fleming agreed.

"I will pay you for your time, Mrs. Fleming. I insist."

"Thank you, Miss Lily. I am lucky, my old man is still in work and he doesn't live in the tavern like many of his friends. But it can be hard to make ends meet. Now, will you have your tea?"

Lily took the glass jar of tea and drank just as if it were a china cup. Bridget did the same. Soon Mike and Tommy were back.

"Thank you, Mrs. Fleming. For everything." Bridget gave the lady a hug.

. . .

"Thank you, Miss Lily, for bringing Bridget back to see us. We are all ever so fond of her, Kathleen, and the little ones. They were a sight for sore eyes on a bad day."

"You should see Kathleen, Mrs. Fleming," Bridget said. "She can sew rings around everyone. Mrs. Wilson, she's in charge of the sewing department, she says Kathleen is good enough to work in one of those stores who dress the rich folks."

"That doesn't surprise me, Bridget. Young Kathleen has always been talented with her needle. Though you, Bridget, have the heart of the whole family. You keep yourself safe, you hear me?"

"Yes, Mrs. Fleming."

"If you ever have need of me, you send a message. I don't care if it's next week or ten years from now. You will always be my friend."

When Lily and the others had gone out the door ahead of her, Bridget found herself wrapped in Mrs. Fleming's arms once more.

"Get yourself out of New York, young Bridget. Miss Lily means well but trust your instinct. It's never let you down"

Bridget hugged her friend back, too choked up to reply. Mrs. Fleming came outside to arrange a time for Lily's friends to drop off the items.

Then they all headed back to the Sanctuary. Tommy made a comment but was greeted with silence so didn't try again. Bridget saw Mini Mike say something to Lily, but she told him to be quiet. She said goodnight to Bridget when they reached the sanctuary and then the group continued to Lily's home. None the wiser as to what Mike had said to Lily, Bridget could only guess it was more bad news.

CHAPTER 9

$\mathcal{A}$ week passed by but there was no word of her brothers. After a restless night's sleep, Bridget had another argument with Maura. Her elder sister was moaning about having to help look after the children who came to the sanctuary during the day while their mothers were working in the sewing rooms. Bridget told Maura she should consider herself lucky to have a job and a roof over her head, which didn't sit well with her elder sister. She had walked off before Maura could reply.

She skipped breakfast and went straight to

the sewing room. It was empty save for Bella, the girl who'd been the least friendly of them all.

"Morning, I thought you would still be at breakfast," Bella said as she shoved something into the folds of her dress.

Was Bella stealing? It was none of her business, so Bridget pretended not to see. She sat at her machine, but instead of sewing her fabric she almost sewed her finger. Hissing, she bit her lip as the tears fell along with the blood. Bella came over to hand her a clean cloth.

"You want to talk?" Bella asked.

"No, thank you."

"Up to you." Bella went back to her seat leaving Bridget feeling bad.

"Sorry Bella. I didn't mean to be rude. I just…things are getting on top of me. I had another argument with my sister this morning and it's left me in bad temper."

"You're lucky," Bella said.

"Me? Why?" Bridget asked.

"Because you have a sister. I ain't got nobody."

Shame filled Bridget as she looked at the other girl more closely. She was about the same age as Kathleen.

"You're right. I shouldn't be moaning, I'm sorry."

"Kathleen is lovely. So pretty and so kind," Bella said.

"Yes, she is," Bridget said. "It wasn't her I was arguing with. It was Maura. She isn't as sweet as Kathleen, but I guess I'm not either."

Bella smiled but didn't respond.

"How long have you been at the sanctuary, Bella? If you don't mind me asking."

"A while. I think it's about eight months now."

"Do you think you will stay here?" Bridget asked.

"There's not much option. Can't think that any man would want me for their bride. Not with how I look."

"You have a lovely face," Bridget said. "And when you smile, your eyes light up."

"It's not my face that worries me," Bella said. "I best get back to work."

Bridget wanted to probe more but the closed look on Bella's face told her not to. Her finger had stopped bleeding, but she wrapped a fragment of cloth around it just in case. She didn't want to damage her work with blood stains. She put the correct material under the needle and started her work for the day. Hopefully she would soon be too distracted to think about her problems.

* * *

"Bridget, could you come to my office please?"

Bridget exchanged a quick look with Kathleen. She gave her sister's hand an encouraging squeeze before following Lily.

"Yes, Lily."

"Kathleen do not be alarmed, your sister

will be back in a little while."

Bridget warmed even more to Lily. She really cared about the people in her care and had noticed Kathleen was concerned.

But she wondered why Lily wanted to speak to her. She brushed her hands down the side of her skirt.

"Come inside and sit down," Lily said.

Bridget had been hovering at the doorway of the beautiful office. The fireplace was set but not lit, given the heat in the day. The wooden desk and chairs shone with lemon polish, the scent mingling with the smell of the various plants dotted around the room. It was cozy and professional at the same time. Lily took a seat on the couch and patted the cushion next to her.

"Cook will bring in some tea in a few minutes as Father Nelson will be joining us. But before he does, I thought we could get to know one another a little. I know we went on a walk the other night, but I didn't get a chance to speak with you. Not properly."

Bridget nodded, her mouth so dry, her tongue stuck to the roof.

"Don't look so worried, Bridget. Nothing you say to me will go outside this office. Why don't I tell you a little bit about me first?"

Bridget listened in wonder as Lily described her life to date. She couldn't believe this well-dressed woman had been so badly abused.

"I am so sorry you had to endure all of that, Lily," Bridget said.

"I didn't tell you my story to ask for pity, but to show you what is possible when you have help from the right people. Father Nelson is very like Father Molloy back in Clover Springs. They are both true Christians who care about their flock. I would love to be able to send you to Clover Springs, but unfortunately, they are currently overwhelmed with new arrivals. The orphanage is overflowing, and new mail order brides have arrived in such numbers, we may have to start sending out mail order husbands." Lily smiled but Bridget couldn't return her smile. "I can tell by the expression on your face, you hadn't given much thought to leaving New York, but I think it may be for the best."

"But why? I thought you said I was safe here." Even as she asked, Bridget remembered Mrs. Fleming had given her the same advice.

"You would be for a while. But we cannot guarantee your safety outside the walls of this building. As you know, Mike said something to me the night of our trip to see Mrs. Fleming. I didn't want to worry you, so I decided to seek my husband's counsel first. I also wanted to speak to him about your brothers. We will wait for Father Nelson to arrive to discuss that further. But with regard to you, Mike heard that not only had Mr. Oaks come looking for you, but he had offered a large reward for you. He wants you returned to his factory."

Bridget gripped the side of the chair tightly.

"We can keep you safe inside of this building, but you are too lovely to spend your time in a prison no matter how it looks on the inside. I want you to listen to what Father Nelson suggests with an open mind. Can you do that?"

Bridget didn't know what else she could do. Lily had presented her with a dilemma. Bridget was sure that spending the rest of her life in the sanctuary wouldn't be that bad at all, but her presence could put the whole project in danger. Not that Lily had said that, but if she couldn't walk outside then Oaks must know where she was. Her family weren't safe either.

"Dearest Bridget, please do not look so frightened." Lily smiled at her reassuringly. "You are among friends here."

The door opened to admit Father Nelson. He was such a big man he immediately made the room feel smaller. Cook followed with a tray of tea and some freshly baked cookies if the smell was anything to go by.

"Good morning Lily. Nice to see you again, Bridget. Isn't it a fine day?"

Bridget couldn't think about the weather. She stared at the priest as if looking at him could tell her his intentions.

CHAPTER 10

*B*ridget waited while Lily and the priest exchanged pleasantries while Lily poured the tea. She took the offered cup, but her hands were shaking so much, Lily took the cup back and placed it on the table beside her. Lily took her hands in hers.

"Bridget, we are your friends," Lily said. "We will not desert you."

Bridget tried to smile but failed miserably.

"Bridget, I can see Lily has already mentioned our concerns about Mr. Oaks. Seems his family is as powerful as you feared. I have spoken to our police friends, but they have discretely suggested it may be safer for everyone if you were to leave New York," Father Nelson said.

"But I have nowhere to go," Bridget said.

"As it happens, you do. But only if you are agreeable."

Bridget listened as Father Nelson spoke of a town called Riverside Springs in Wyoming State. It was in desperate need of good women who would help settle the new State. He suggested she and Maura go as mail order brides.

"You mean I'd have to marry someone I've never met?" Bridget asked.

"Yes, but it's not as bad as it seems," Father Nelson said. "Rather than place an advert in one of the many periodicals and marry a stranger, as most do, our way is better. We have a good friend living in the town."

"Reverend Franklin wouldn't let you marry a man who isn't kind and decent," Lily interrupted.

"A God-fearing man," Father Nelson said.

"We're not encouraging you to go all that way to marry a man who spends his nights in the saloon."

"But what of my family? Maura, Kathleen, the young ones?" Bridget asked.

"The police feel Oaks is only interested in you, so the rest of your family should be safe. The older girls can work here in the sanctuary or make a similar decision to the one you have been offered. The younger ones, well, that is another subject. Should we ask Maura to join us? She is your elder sister, isn't she? And, therefore, responsible for the family?" Lily asked.

"Yes, she is, but given her recent tragedy, Maura is not herself." Maura had always been self-centered, but Bridget wasn't about to admit that.

"Forgive my bluntness, Bridget, but you have all suffered. Let Maura share the burden of your siblings. We do not have sufficient space or resources at the sanctuary to house young children for a long period of time. There are places in New York for orphans, but we feel they may not provide the best solution," Lily said firmly before she rang a bell and cook appeared. "Can you ask Maura to join us please."

"Yes ma'am."

Maura soon arrived and, Bridget could see by her white face, her sister wasn't in her right mind. She sat beside Bridget, grabbing her hand as if she would never let go.

"Maura, I have just been discussing your younger siblings with Bridget. It is our suggestion that you allow the children to be adopted. Father Nelson is very involved with the Out-placement Society, a charity that helps place children in homes around the country.

"You mean to put them on the orphan train?" Maura asked.

"Well, yes, that is the name the papers have given to the arrangement. The children would be placed in loving homes and given the best start possible in life," Lily said.

"But that means we would never see them

again," Maura wailed. "How can you do that? Haven't we lost enough?"

"Maura, calm yourself," Bridget said. "Lily and Father Nelson are trying to help. How can we keep the children? They can't continue living here. You don't have a job, and I can't live in New York. We have no other option."

"But, Bridget, we promised Mam."

"I know, but Mam would understand. Living on the streets wondering where the next penny is coming from isn't the life Mam wanted for her family. She didn't want us to be subjected to these types of abuse and corruption. Look at the state of Michael and Shane. They are in the Tombs for goodness sake. They are already doing things Mam would have given them …" Bridget stopped herself just in time. The twinkle in Father Nelson's eyes suggested he knew what she had been about to say.

"We will discuss Michael and Shane in a minute, but for now we must have an answer on what you intend to do," Lily said.

"Us?" Maura looked around her, a panicked expression on her face.

"Lily and Father Nelson have suggested we consider becoming mail order brides," Bridget said.

"Me, marry a stranger? After everything I've been through? Never. How could you even suggest it? You know how much I loved David."

Bridget bit back her temper. Yes, Maura had been through a lot, but life hadn't exactly been a bed of roses for her either. But her sister couldn't see beyond herself.

"Yes, but he's gone," Bridget said. "You're alive. What are you going to do?"

"I will become a nun before I marry a stranger," Maura said.

"That can be arranged, Maura, but I suggest you give the idea some more thought. A calling to the priesthood or religious orders, while wonderful, is a lifetime decision. Not one to be made on the spur of the moment," Father Nelson added.

Maura stood and ran from the room.

"I apologize for my sister," Bridget said. "She hasn't been right since her fiancé was killed."

"Don't worry. We will look after Maura, but what about you, Bridget? Do you think you could become a mail order bride?" Lily asked, a kind but thoughtful expression on her face.

"Could my siblings be sent to the same area?" Bridget asked.

Lily exchanged a look with Father Nelson.

"We might be able to arrange that," Father Nelson said doubtfully. "But if they are adopted, Bridget, their new families may discourage all contact."

She would deal with it when it happened. If she could keep her family together until they got to Riverside Springs, maybe she would find an alternative.

"I would like to be with them for as long as possible," Bridget said.

"You may be putting off the inevitable and increasing your pain," Father Nelson said.

"Thank you, Father, but I don't think that is possible. After the last few weeks, my family need me."

She saw the priest and Lily exchange a look, but she didn't care. She had bought herself some time and that was all that mattered.

"What will happen to Michael and Shane?" she asked next.

"They are still underage, but as they are orphans, I can arrange for them to be released and placed on one of the trains. I have spoken to friends on the force and they said their so-called crimes amount to little more than petty thieving." Father Nelson took a deep breath. "While I never condone stealing, I can understand how hunger would tempt a man, never mind a child. If we get them on the trains they will have a chance."

"But who will adopt older boys?" Bridget asked.

"It's highly unlikely they will be adopted, Bridget. As you imagine, the majority of children who are adopted tend to be the younger ones. The older boys are often taken in by farming families to help on the land. They will receive schooling where possible and will be able to leave when they are twenty-one. At that time, they will receive their wages and a suit of clothes."

"Would they be treated kindly?" Bridget asked.

The look in the priest eyes made her shudder.

"I would love to tell you, yes, and believe it with my whole heart. But I cannot say that with certainty. What I can say, is that we do our best to find good homes for all the children. And I can safely say that being out in the fresh air learning a trade and way of life will be a thousand times better than existing in their current environment. If they survive the Tombs they are likely to be hardened criminals on their release."

"Yes, Father," Bridget said. "Send them on the trains."

"You don't want to discuss this with Maura?" Lily asked.

"She will agree," Bridget said. "You do what you think best. We are very grateful for your help. Can I write them a note before they go?"

"Yes, of course you may. I will take it to them myself," Father Nelson said. "I have asked that they be released into the care of the local asylum. I will go and see them in the next day or two."

"Thank you, Father. They are good boys, or at least they were until they got mixed up with the gangs. I pray that they would find their way back to God and us with the help of strangers."

"We will all pray for that, Bridget. Won't we, Lily?"

CHAPTER 11

RIVERSIDE SPRINGS WYOMING

*B*rian Curran pushed the hair out of his eyes. Despite being stripped to the waist, the sweat ran down his arms. The hot summer sun beat down so hard, it was a wonder the field of hay didn't catch fire. He pulled out his flask and swallowed a drink of water.

"Hey Mitch, we almost done? I think I'm being broiled alive."

"Nearly. If we get this finished, we can start fresh on the top field tomorrow."

Brian grunted in reply. He didn't have the energy to argue with his friend. Mitch had given him his first job when he'd finished his indenture all those years ago. Since then they had become close, almost like brothers. Mitch had encouraged Brian to pursue his dream of running his own place. He'd helped him lay claim to his land. The least he could do was help Mitch with his crop. He was short of hands as he couldn't get cash from the bank to pay for his casual workers. With the big banks closing, the smaller town banks wouldn't lend any money even if you offered to secure the loan with gold coins.

"You're coming back to the house for dinner, right? Shannon has enough for all of us," Mitch said.

"I bet she has," Brian muttered. He liked his friend's wife, but she was too keen on marrying Brian off for his liking. She kept harping on about using a catalogue of mail order brides. Just because her and Mitch had met that way and now had a very happy marriage didn't mean it was suitable for everyone. Brian was quite happy on his own. At least, that's what he told himself.

He couldn't remember having a family. Not a real one anyway. His days back in New York were a long distant memory. After a brief time spent in the children's hospital, he'd left on one of the so-called Orphan Trains. The Moores had provided him with lodgings, food, and some schooling in return for his labor. But he was never considered part of the family. They didn't even offer him the chance to stay on as a laborer once his indenture period was over. They gave him his money and his suit as promised and wished him well. Then they headed off to meet the next fifteen-year-old lad who would put in six years of labor on their farm.

Brian closed his eyes, remembering how he had headed to his bed in the barn while the family had slept in the house. It wasn't appropriate for him to share with the girls of the family, but he would have happily shared Tom's room. But Mr. Moore wouldn't hear of the orphan sharing with his son. Brian had stood watching in from the window as the family had gathered around the fire, telling stories, swapping tales of their day at school. Mrs. Moore, a kindly soul much in awe of her husband, knitting by the fire with the girls, Julia and Samantha, at her feet. Tom perched on his father's right-hand side. Brian would watch them laughing and joking, wishing they would include him. When they prayed together he folded his hands in prayer, joining in as he learned the words. Only they never knew. Somehow, he'd known they wouldn't appreciate him eavesdropping on their family time.

Brian ducked as Mitch's arm nearly hit his head.

"You back with us yet, or are you still lollygagging?" Mitch asked.

"Sorry, Mitch," Brian said, shaking his head to clear his thoughts. "How about a race?

Whoever finishes first gets the biggest slice of pie after dinner."

"You're on," Mitch replied, grinning.

Brian threw himself into the work. Breaking a sweat was better than breaking his heart over old hurts. Six years he had been away from the Moores. More than long enough for those wounds to heal.

They finished the work in record time and sat in the field, enjoying a drink of water.

"Brian, I know the missus annoys you with her chatter about you getting wed. It's only because she's lonely. You know there are few women around her. It would be nice for Shannon to have some new friends. Mrs. Clarke and Mrs. Peoples are nice, but they are that much older. If you were to wed, Shannon would gain a friend, someone to talk to about all that women's stuff."

Brian stared at the ground, but he was listening.

"It would be good for you too. There's nothing like coming home to a hot meal and even nicer company. I don't know where I would be without my Shannon."

"Starving and cold?" Brian joked.

"I'm serious Brian. You are too nice a guy to live alone."

CHAPTER 12

RIVERSIDE SPRINGS WYOMING

Brian rode into Riverside Springs. The town was quieter than usual, it being a Sunday morning. The people would start arriving for services shortly, but he wanted a bit of quiet time in the church. He wanted to talk to God about his future and Mitch's suggestion he find a mail order bride.

"Good morning Brian. Bit early for you today, isn't it? I don't see any wedding and it's not Christmas."

Brian didn't react to the Reverend's teasing. They both knew he wasn't a regular church goer.

"Morning Reverend Franklin. Yes, I was hoping to get some time alone. I felt it was right to come here." Although he couldn't explain why he was drawn to the church so hoped the Reverend wouldn't ask.

"You have a lot on your mind?" the reverend asked, "Want to talk about it?"

Brian didn't but to say so would be rude. Reverend Franklin was a kindly old soul. Nobody knew what age he was but if he had to guess, Brian thought he was about sixty.

"A problem shared and all that," the reverend prompted.

"Mitch thinks it is time I found myself a wife," Brian said.

"And you don't?"

"No, well yes. Oh, I don't know. There are no women around these parts. Not ones you want to marry," Brian said.

"Mitch and Shannon are happy, aren't they?" Reverend Franklin asked.

"Yes, but what if Mitch just got lucky? What if the woman who comes here for me looks like a …"

"Now Brian, you should know better. It is not how someone looks on the outside but the inside that counts. Her heart and her faith. Everything else comes second."

That was easy for Reverend Franklin to say. He wouldn't have to live with whoever came looking for a husband. What was wrong with her that finding one in New York was so difficult? Surely there had to be plenty of single men out there?

"As it happens, I have had a letter from a good friend of mine by the name of Thomas Nelson. Father Nelson, yes, he is a catholic priest, is involved with a lady's sanctuary. He has written of a delightful young girl by the name of Bridget who finds herself in need of a husband."

A women's sanctuary. What type of place was that? Was she a criminal?

"This young lady has been a victim of a

rather unscrupulous man. The man in question is wealthy and seems to believe the young ladies who work for him are his property. According to Father Nelson, he treats them little better than slaves," Reverend Franklin said.

"Women having to work hard is hardly a crime, is it?" Brian asked.

"It is when the person they work for expects them to provide additional services."

Brian stared at the ground, his cheeks burning. He couldn't say anything. What type of man would force himself on a young girl?

"This girl, Bridget Collins, defended herself and in the process hurt the owner's son."

"Good for her," Brian replied.

"Maybe, but maybe not. The man wants to press charges and so far, hasn't been able to as Bridget is being protected. But Father Nelson believes she would be better leaving New York as soon as possible. She needs a good man to marry and protect her."

Brian rubbed his finger inside his collar. It was hot outside, but he had a chill running down his backbone. The way the reverend was looking at him, he was expecting Brian to volunteer to marry this young woman. He hadn't even seen a picture of her.

"It would be an act of charity," Reverend Franklin said. "To save a young devout woman from injustice. You could say God directed you here this morning in answer to this young lady's prayers."

Brian wished he had volunteered to check the herd rather than come early into town.

"I don't know, Reverend. I haven't fully decided to marry. What if we don't get on?" he asked.

"All marriages have their trials. All relationships do, if we are honest. Do you not think there are days when being a man of God is the last thing I want to be?"

Brian couldn't hide his shock.

"Yes, young man," the reverend said, laughing slightly. "I, too, had dreams of living another life. But God calls, and we have to answer him. You do not have to marry young

Bridget straight away. You could send for her and she can live with someone, maybe Shannon and Mitch until such a time as you both feel ready to marry."

Brian liked the sound of that. If she arrived and looked like a mule, he didn't have to get wed.

"Of course, there would be certain expectations but no doubt in time you would come to see the inner beauty and not just the surrounding package."

How could the Reverend do that? How could he read his mind so easily?

"Yes Reverend."

"Good, then I will write to Father Nelson immediately after services and tell him. I will need you to write a letter too."

"Me?" Brian asked. "Why?"

"To your intended," Reverend Franklin said. "Tell her a little about yourself. The poor woman is going to travel halfway across the country to marry a stranger. It would be nice if you could tell her a little bit about yourself, wouldn't it?"

Brian nodded, feeling a little sick. He had just agreed to marry a stranger. And all he had come in for was a quiet chat with his creator. God did work in mysterious ways, that was for sure.

He paced up and down wondering what he should write. Then he sat and sucked the pencil waiting for inspiration. The time ticked by. At this rate, Reverend Franklin would have to write the letter for him. Or maybe he would ask Shannon to write it, her being a lady. That was too embarrassing to think about, so Brian started scribbling.

DEAR MISS. COLLINS

Reverend Franklin has suggested I write and offer you a marriage proposal. As you can see, writing and talking to women isn't my strong point.

I am almost twenty-seven years old. I have

my own piece of land, some crops, and some animals, set in the prettiest place on earth. I live just north of Riverside Springs.

Riverside Springs is a small but growing town. It's peaceful. Maybe some would consider it too quiet, but I like it. My nearest neighbor and best friend is married to a fine lady by the name of Shannon.

I believe you have to leave New York quickly but if you do get a chance to reply, I look forward to your letter.

Yours ...

BRIAN SUCKED THE PENCIL. How should he sign off the letter? It wasn't particularly romantic was it? But then how could it be when all he knew about the girl was her name.

"All done, Brian?" Reverend Franklin came back to the church.

Brian gathered it was time for services.

"Have you the letter ready? I don't want to miss David Dunne." The reverend held out his hand. "He is riding up to Green River and agreed to put the post on the train for me."

Brian handed the Reverend the letter, only realizing later he had never signed it. Miss Collins would think he was some greenhorn. Maybe she would find an alternative match.

CHAPTER 13

NEW YORK

*L*ily walked into the sewing room early one afternoon.

"Bridget, I've had a message from Mrs. Fleming. She has asked me to come and see her. Would you like to come with me? Mike and Tommy will be with us."

"Yes, please. I would love to get to say goodbye to Mrs. Fleming before I leave New York. She was very good to me, to all of us."

"Good, we will go this evening."

* * *

IN THE SUMMER HEAT, the tenements smelled worse than the markets. Crippled beggars fought with women and children, hawking anything from fruit to newspapers. It took time to walk down the streets and dark alley especially as people stopped to say hello to Lily at every turn. Bridget watched her in awe as she greeted everyone with the same smile. The woman never ceased to amaze her; the love and consideration she shared for those less fortunate was truly amazing to see.

Mrs. Fleming was waiting outside her rooms. "Bridget, you look like a proper lady. Don't you scrub up nice?"

Blushing, Bridget guessed it was a rhetorical question as Mrs. Fleming kept talking.

"Miss Lily, thank ya for coming down so quickly. There's a couple of children who need help. Jacob Kelly and his younger sister Lizzie. I've been feeding them the last few days but much as I would love to take them in, I just don't have the room."

"Where are they? Where are their parents?" Bridget asked.

"Their ma, God rest her, died having her latest babe. The child didn't last five minutes. Their Pa, "Mrs. Fleming screwed up her face in distaste, "the coppers took him away. After all these years and those poor dead children. They finally saw him for the murdering varmint he was."

"The police didn't think to take the children to safety?" Lily asked, her face white.

"I don't think they knew about them. Jacob took Lizzie to hide from their Pa when he went on his latest rampage. That young fella, he's been protecting the child since the day she was born. Only for him, she'd been dead too. They didn't come back until their Pa was long gone."

"Oh, God love them, the poor children. Where are they? Of course, we will take them." Lily looked around as if expecting the children to materialize.

Mrs. Fleming led them to a room further

inside the tenement, it was smaller than the one they had lived in.

A young boy with a hard stare stood at the door, his face marked by an ugly red scar running from the outer corner of his eye to his mouth. Bridget couldn't contain the gasp of horror, but Lily didn't show any reaction. She walked toward the boy who stepped back, walking backward until he came to a pile of rags on the floor. He lashed out catching Lily unawares, his leg connecting with her skirts. Bridget winced on her new friend's behalf as Lily paled.

"Jacob stop it, this lady is here to help ya. She is an angel. Have you not heard of Lily Doherty?" Mrs. Fleming hissed.

The boy's eyes widened but he made no move to stand down. The pile of rags moved, a whimpering sound announcing it was a small child.

Lily crouched down so she was smaller than the boy. "Jacob, I am not going to hurt you. I want to help you and Lizzie. I am sorry about your Ma and the baby."

"Who says you won't give us back to him?" the boy demanded, his body stiff.

"Him?" Lily queried softly.

"Pa. He told me he'd kill us sooner than let us go."

"Oh, child, your Pa can't touch you now. The police have him, and from what Mrs. Fleming told me, he will be staying in jail for a very long time." Lily inched closer to him, but he continued to watch her warily. Mrs. Fleming looked at Bridget, she could see the tears in the older woman's eyes.

"Will you come with me? I have a house full of women and children. Bridget, the lady with me, her brother and sister live there. Don't they, Bridget?"

Bridget didn't get a chance to respond. Mrs. Fleming moved toward the boy instead.

"Yes, they do, Jacob. I know Bridget well, she used to live beside me. Maybe you re-member her brother Liam and young Annie with the head of blonde curls on her. She looks like a little angel."

Jacob shook his head.

"Mrs. Fleming wouldn't let you come with us unless she trusted me, would she?" Lily asked.

Jacob looked to Mrs. Fleming quickly before staring back at Lily. It took him a few minutes but finally he shook his head. Bridget watched Lily closely, not wanting to say anything in case it upset the boy.

"Will you introduce us to Lizzie?"

Jacob's eyes didn't leave Lily's face as he bent down to pull the young girl to her feet. His touch was so gentle. Bridget had been expecting him to drag her to her feet, but he didn't. He showed more patience than most adults would have in a similar situation. Lizzie, a very pretty little girl, clung to Jacob's side, her thumb in her mouth, eyes wide, darting from Bridget to Lily to Mrs. Fleming and back again.

"Nice to meet you Lizzie. My name is Lily,

and this is Bridget. Would you like to come with us? The sanctuary is safe and there are children who would love to play with you."

The girl blinked rapidly, indecision written all over her face. Her eyes darted to her brother's face and then back to Lily.

"Can Jacob stay with me?"

"Of course, he can. The both of you are welcome."

Lizzie gazed up at her brother, the look of adoration on her face bringing a tear to Bridget's eye. She blinked rapidly, not wanting to upset anyone by bursting into tears. At least Annie and Liam had been spared the cruelty inflicted on these poor children.

"We'll come, but I don't know if we will be staying. We got family outside New York. We were planning on heading out to their place." Jacob's tone sounded confident but his eyes darting from one side of the room to the other gave him away.

Bridget caught Mrs. Flemings slight shake of her head. She guessed Lily knew the boy was lying too but she didn't let on. Instead Lily went along with what he had said. "That's fine, Jacob. When you both have had a good meal and a hot bath, we can discuss your plans. Maybe we can help you reach your family."

The children were filthy and so thin, their skin was almost translucent.

"Jacob, is there anything you need to bring with you?"

"No. I have everything right here." He pointed to Lizzie. She was still holding onto his hand as if expecting him to disappear.

"Right, shall we go? Thank you so much Mrs. Fleming. We will be in contact soon. This way children."

Lily led the way out of the building with Bridget and Mrs. Fleming bringing up the rear behind the children. Bridget told her quickly about her plans to leave New York as a mail order bride.

"Promise me you will write to me, Bridget. I want to hear from your own mouth you are happy."

"I will Mrs. Fleming. Thank you for everything you did for my family."

"Our kind must stick together. It's the only way any of us survive." Mrs. Fleming looked at the children as she spoke.

"What happened to Jacob's face?" Bridget asked in a whisper, so the child wouldn't hear her.

"He stopped his Pa from beating Lizzie. Fred didn't like it. No adult ever stood up to Fred never mind a ten-year-old boy. He took his belt off and battered the child with it. Nearly killed him."

"Oh, the poor boy. Didn't anyone help him?"

"Nobody wanted to interfere, did they? I didn't know the family back then. I would have sent my boys around to give that Fred a taste of his own medicine. He murdered his other children, so they say. His wife too."

"I thought she died in childbirth."

"That's what they told young Jacob. It's kinder than telling him the truth. The child has been through enough." Mrs. Fleming hugged Bridget close again before turning away and walking quickly back toward the tenement. Bridget watched her go, thinking the woman had the biggest heart. Not that many got to see it with her gruff exterior.

"Don't fall behind Miss Bridget, stay up front with Lily. That way we know we haven't lost you." Tommy gave her a reassuring look but after his reminder, she'd be glad to be back inside the sanctuary.

CHAPTER 14

"*B*ridget, could I leave you to settle Lizzie and Jacob? I have to get home to speak to Charlie about something."

"Of course, Lily. See you in the morning. Come on children, you must be hungry."

The children didn't answer but followed her, their eyes widening as they looked around the building. Lizzie moved closer to Jacob. Annie came running down the stairs, closely followed by Liam.

"Bridget, thank goodness you are back.

Maura is in a foul mood again." Liam slid to a halt. "Who are you?" he asked Jacob.

"Liam Collins, is that any way to greet our new guests?" Bridget reprimanded her brother gently. "This is Jacob and his sister Lizzie. They are friends of Mrs. Fleming but have come to stay with us here at the sanctuary for a little while."

"It's great here. Well, they make you take baths and stuff, but the food is good." Liam spoke to Jacob, but the boy stared right through him.

Annie moved toward Lizzie. "Would you like to hold my doll? Bridget made it for me?" she asked the little girl. Lizzie put her hand out hesitantly but at a sharp look from Jacob let it fall to her side.

"We don't need nothing from no one," Jacob replied on his sister's behalf. "Leave us be."

Bridget wanted to hug Annie as the little girl's eyes filled with tears.

"Don't you speak to my sister like that. She

was only trying to be nice. Come on Annie, let's go back to Kathleen. She said she will tell us a story until Bridget comes up."

Bridget hid her pride in her brother's concern for his sister. He was such a lovely young boy with a huge heart. His unkindness to Jacob was a cover for his own hurt.

"Come on Lizzie, Jacob. Let's see what Cook has to eat." Bridget forced her voice to sound cheerful, leading the children through to the kitchen. Cook had the evening off but there was plenty of food to make up two cold plates. While the children ate, Bridget told them she would take them upstairs to have a bath and then show them where they would sleep.

"Lizzie, you will sleep in the girl's room and Jacob will be in the boy's room right next door."

"We sleep together."

Bridget met the boy's eyes. "I don't think that is possible Jacob, but I promise you Lizzie will be well looked after. You are both safe here. Nobody is going to hurt you."

He didn't believe her, it was evident from his expression. She busied herself around the kitchen as they finished their meal pretending not to notice as he filled his pockets with the leftovers.

"Come on both of you. I am tired and need my bed. I am sure you are too. Lizzie, will you have the first bath?"

Lizzie shrunk away from her, her little hand reaching for her brother.

"Jacob can't come in with you to the bath-room, but he can stand right outside. Is that all right?"

Lizzie looked terrified. To her surprise Jacob bent down and spoke to the little girl in such a kind voice, Bridget couldn't believe it was the same boy.

"I will be right outside. You scream if you are scared and I will burst right in. I won't leave, I promise."

Lizzie didn't reply but stared at him, her large blue eyes swimming in tears. She continued to stare at him even when the door closed, and she could no longer see her brother.

"Lizzie, let me take your clothes. They need to be burned," Bridget said softly as she slowly undressed the little girl, biting her lip not to cry out at the numerous marks on the child's body. Not only was she way too thin but some of the injuries she had received had left scars.

"Is the water all right? Not too hot?"

Lizzie didn't reply. She just sat miserably in the middle of the tub. Bridget chatted casually as she washed years of grime from the little girl's body, careful not to hurt her. She then washed her hair twice. She used the evil smelling concoction Mrs. Wilson swore by for dealing with lice. She should really cut the child's hair, but she figured that was one trauma too many for the little one to deal with.

"Your hair is beautiful Lizzie, such a lovely color. Did your ma have hair like it?"

Lizzie didn't answer but continued to stare

into the water. If she hadn't heard her speak to Jacob, she would think she was mute.

Once the child was clean and the water filthy, Bridget wrapped her in a towel and proceeded to dry her.

"You all right, Lizzie?" Jacob's voice came from behind the door. Bridget hurried to dress the little girl before she opened the door to reassure him his sister was fine. His eyes searched past her and widened as he stared at the child.

"Lizzie, is that you?"

Lizzie smiled before she nodded. She held her hands out for a hug, but he took a step back. "I will only get you dirty again."

"Jacob, I have run your bath and will come back in a few minutes to do your hair. I will put Lizzie to bed in the girl's dormitory." At the mulish expression on his face, she insisted. "you can go visit her when you are washed. Now go on, the water is getting cold."

Bridget led Lizzie to the girl's room where

Kathleen was waiting with Annie. There was no sign of Liam.

"Annie thought Lizzie might be a little scared, so she wanted to come to say goodnight."

Bridget picked up her little sister and cuddled her close

"That was nice of you Annie."

"I thought I could tell her a story like you tell me."

Bridget nodded, her throat clogging as Annie reached for Lizzie's hand. "Come up here onto this bed. I will read you a story, so you don't have to be afraid."

Lizzie took Annie's hand and with a little help from Kathleen climbed onto the bed. Bridget left her sisters with Lizzie as she headed back to the bathroom to deal with Jacob.

He complained as she walked in.

"You shouldn't be in here."

"Whist will you? You will scare the children. I have three brothers of my own Jacob.

Now let me do your hair." Having decided she needed to show the child who was in charge, Bridget adopted a firm tone. It took all her concentration especially when she saw the state of his body. He made Lizzie look well cared for. She was glad she hadn't met his father as if he was responsible for the weals and scars crisscrossing the child's body, she would find it difficult to restrain herself.

"Jacob, I need to shave your head. It will help get rid of the itching and will grow back quickly."

He didn't argue with her but shrank away as she came closer. "I promise I won't hurt you, but you have to be still."

He shook a little when she started but soon seemed to realize she wasn't going to torture him. Soon he was finished. Unlike Lizzie he looked worse than when he had first arrived. The dirt had managed to hide some of the physical scars inflicted on his body, the shaved head highlighted the wound on his face. She wondered if a doctor could do anything to help and resolved to speak to Lily first thing in the morning.

"I will leave you to get dressed. There are clean clothes right here."

"Where are you taking my stuff?"

"They will have to be burnt."

As his face fell, her heart nearly broke. "Jacob, the new clothes are yours to keep. No matter how long you stay here. There is plenty of food too. I know you find it difficult to believe but nobody here is going to harm you. I promise."

She wanted to hug him close but sensed he wouldn't like it. Taking his pathetic pile of belongings, she left the room and headed down to the furnace wishing she could add all the adults who had mistreated the child so badly to the same pile.

When she came back, Jacob was standing outside the bathroom, his wary expression watching her every move.

"Sorry Jacob, couldn't you find the boy's

room? I thought I showed it to you before you took your bath?"

"Where is Lizzie?"

"She is in the girl's room."

"I want to see her."

Bridget knew it was against the rules but sometimes rules were meant to be broken.

"You will have to be very quiet. Come with me." She led the way into the girl's dormitory to Lizzie's bed. Smiling, she saw the child was fast asleep, Annie's rag doll clutched tightly to her chest.

"See, she is sleeping. She is perfectly safe. Now let me show you again where your bed is."

Jacob opened his mouth but shut it again. Maybe he had decided there wasn't any point in arguing. He leaned over and brushed the hair from Lizzie's face then followed Bridget. She led the way in silence to his room.

"You can sleep here. The two boys sleeping are Eddie and his friend Danny. They arrived yesterday. Would you like the door closed?"

He shook his head and for a split second she saw his fear-filled eyes.

"Jacob, I will leave the light on. I sleep on the next floor. If you need me for anything, come knock on my door."

He didn't respond but sat on the bed staring at his hands. She wondered what else she could say to reassure him but, in the end, decided it was best if she proved he was safe.

SHE WOKE EARLY the next morning and went to check on Jacob. His bed was empty causing her heart to hammer faster. Had he run away? She quickly went to check on Lizzie and there on the floor by his sister's bed was Jacob curled into a ball, sleeping soundly despite the obviously uncomfortable sleeping arrangement. She pulled the door closed, not wanting to wake him or the other children. Let them enjoy their dreams for a little while longer.

CHAPTER 15

*B*ridget straightened up a bit in her chair. Her shoulders ached from the hours over the sewing machine, but it was so much easier than the work she had done back in the laundry. Kathleen had turned into something of a teacher's pet with Mrs. Wilson continuously praising her work. Bridget was glad to see her younger sister regaining her confidence. It was a good thing Kathleen was so sweet-natured or the other women might have picked on her. But she was so nice to everyone, the other women didn't mind the constant praise.

Maura, on the other hand, was not fitting in well at the sanctuary at all. Her continuous criticism and finding fault with everything was wearing thin even for her sisters. She was supposed to be helping by teaching the children and keeping them occupied while the others worked but it didn't seem to appeal to Maura.

Bridget had walked in on her shouting at Jacob saying he had to make more of an effort on his letters. The boy's surly face suggested Maura was wasting her voice. When Bridget got a chance later to ask the boy how his school work was going, she found out he had never attended school so barely knew how to write his own name.

"Pa said there was no need for a mutton-head like me to learn letters. Reading and writing isn't for the likes of us."

"Oh Jacob, you couldn't be more wrong. Learning to read and write will help you to find better work and be able to provide a good living for your family." Bridget nearly fell over as the child reared on her.

"What family? You are going to take Lizzie away from me. I know you are, and you can't deny it."

"Jacob calm down. Nobody is going to take Lizzie anywhere. Whatever gave you that idea?"

"Your sister. She said we were going on a train and they would give us to different people. Lizzie would have a new Ma and Pa. Nobody would want me."

Thankful Maura had decided to walk to the store for Cook, Bridget took a deep breath. She couldn't lie to the child, but she had to do something to lessen the damage her sister's uncaring comments had caused.

"Jacob, sit down and talk to me. I promise to tell you the truth but only if we discuss it properly. I won't let you shout at me. That is not how we communicate."

Jacob glared at her, but she just stared back at him until he took a seat.

"It's true that the plan is to put you and Lizzie on the so-called orphan train but..." Bridget held up her hand, "our hope is to find a home for both of you. We don't want to separate you and Lizzie, but you can't go on living here. This place was designed to provide shelter to young women rather than children. Anyway, wouldn't you like to have a new home in the country? With fresh air and good food?"

"I ain't a kid."

Bridget wanted to point out he was only ten, but his challenging stare warned her not to. She remained silent.

"I can get a job and look after Lizzie. Nobody is going to want me, are they? Not with the way I look."

"They will when they get to know you. You have the heart of a lion and your love for Lizzie is a joy to watch. Any parents would be proud to have you in their family."

He watched her under his lashes for a few seconds before abruptly pushing the table back as he stood up. "I like you, Miss Bridget, but you believe in fairy tales. Real life ain't like that."

He was gone before she could respond. She stood to follow him only to meet her sister coming back from her walk.

"I hope you are here to help. Nobody told me you and Lily were going to take in more orphans, just how many children do you expect me to look after?"

"If I had my way Maura Collins, I wouldn't let you look after a dog."

Bridget didn't wait for a response but walked swiftly away, her hands clenched by her side. Her sister would try the patience of a saint and she was far from that.

Later that morning, Bridget bit her lip as Lily called her down to the office. As she walked into the room, she saw a letter on the table.

"Here you are Bridget, this one is for you," Lily said, motioning toward the letter.

Bridget looked at it, then back to Lily.

"Go on, open it. It can't bite you."

Bridget picked up the letter with shaking hands. She opened it and began to read. The man couldn't even be bothered to sign his name. He obviously thought she was desperate. He wasn't wrong.

She let the letter fall to the table.

"Oh dear. Was he not pleasant?" Lily asked. "Reverend Franklin wrote to speak highly of him. Said he was a quiet man, but respectful and a good Christian."

"He's not Catholic."

"No, he isn't, but given the circumstances we can't be picky" Lily said. "Father Nelson and Reverend Franklin are good friends."

Bridget looked back at the letter. He might be God-fearing, but he was still rude. She gave the letter to Lily.

"Here, read it for yourself," Bridget said.

Lily read the letter, and, to Bridget's surprise, she smiled.

"What?"

"It's a lovely letter, Bridget. What a nice man."

"Nice? He didn't even sign his name," Bridget said.

"I know, but doesn't that just show you he is as nervous as you are?" Lily asked. "His name is Brian Curran. Reverend Franklin wrote about him in glowing terms. Men have feelings just the same as women do. Some of them lack confidence. Maybe his folks weren't the kind to tell him he was wonderful."

Bridget stared at Lily and then took the letter. This time she read it with what Lily said in mind. He mentioned he didn't know how to talk to women. So, he was shy and maybe a little bit lonely despite his talk of the place being quiet. He appreciated nature as he said the area they lived in was beautiful. A small town would be totally different to the bustling streets of New York.

"So, decision time, Bridget," Lily said. "What are you going to do?"

"I would like to go but I want to take Annie

and young Liam with me. I am sure they could find homes in a small town like Riverside Springs. Don't you think so?"

Lily looked uncertain. Suddenly Bridget thought she was going to say no.

"Please ma'am, I mean Lily, don't make me go without them. The poor children can't depend on Maura to look after them. Kathleen is young, and she deserves to have a happy future."

"So, do you Bridget. You cannot put your family ahead of your own happiness all the time."

"But the children; they are only four and six," Bridget said. "If I don't look out for them, who will?"

"All right, Bridget. You can take the children with you but on one condition. If you do not find them suitable homes, you must return them to the sanctuary and allow Father Nelson to place them. Is that clear?" Lily asked.

"Yes, Lily. I have the money for their fares."

"How?"

"I have my wages. I was going to use them for some clothes, but it is best to bring the children," Bridget said.

"I will pay for the children's tickets. You use your money to buy some necessities for your trip. I hope everything works out for you, Bridget. You deserve to find happiness." Lily stood up and clasped Bridget close in a hug. "Remember to be as kind to yourself as you are to others."

CHAPTER 16

*A*s it turned out Father Nelson had a better idea.

"Bridget, Lily has told me of your plan. I think it is risky to believe there will be a family, or families, in Riverside Springs to take on your siblings. But, before you interrupt," Father Nelson said, waving his hand as if he knew exactly what she was about to do.

Bridget closed her mouth and sat on her hands, so she wouldn't interrupt.

"I have a proposition for you," he went on. "I need a young woman of impeccable character to accompany a trainload of orphans on their journey. The lady who was due to travel has fallen ill and her father insists she remain at home. You are perfect to take her place. Your role will be to ensure the safety of the children while traveling. We don't want to lose any."

"That was an unfortunate incident, Father. It only happened the one time and she was found eventually," Lily added.

Bridget looked at Lily who explained a little girl had been left behind at a stop and the train had to wait until she was found.

"The poor little mite was out of her mind," Lily said.

"I can just imagine." Bridget didn't show any fear at taking the train, but she wasn't excited about the prospect. She knew New York, the bad and the good. But she knew nothing of the world outside of it.

"Yes. So, you can see the need for proper supervision," Father Nelson said. "The boys will have a male supervisor. We can introduce you to him when I find out which man is traveling this time."

"So, Annie and Liam can come along with me?" Bridget asked, her tone suggesting she wouldn't go without them.

"The train travels to a number of places before Green River. That is the last stop. If you have not found suitable homes for Liam and Annie by then, you will have to take a chance on Riverside Springs. But, and this is meant for your own good, Bridget, I would suggest you try your best to have the children settled prior to reaching your final destination."

"I will, Father." Bridget crossed her fingers under her skirt. She wasn't giving up her siblings to anyone.

"Good. You will be paid for your time and obviously the board of the Outplacement Society will cover the cost of the train journeys. The railways are good to us. They give us a huge discount on the children's fares." Father Nelson smiled at her, but Bridget was too upset to do anything but stare at him.

CHAPTER 17

*B*rian rode up the main street and was about to dismount when Mr. Grayson, the storekeeper, appeared on his porch. "Brian, letter for you. Came all the way from New York."

Brian hid his face from anyone watching. It was a huge drawback, living in such a small town where everyone knew each other's business. It would be all over the local community that he had been writing letters to a gal in New York.

The letter, well, note would be a better description, confirmed Bridget Collins would be here in a couple of months. She was working for a children's group called the Outplacement Society, escorting a trainload of orphans along the route to Green River. Once her charges had been placed with their families, she would travel onto Riverside Springs to get married.

He wiped the sweat from his eyes. There was nothing about her in the letter, only that she had agreed to their marriage. He didn't know if she was four feet ten with brown hair or six feet tall with red hair. Surely, she could have added some personal details. Maybe she didn't like writing. He folded the letter and put it into his pocket. Now wasn't the time to start speculating on her motives. He had work to do and lollygagging around here wasn't going to get it done.

"So, I heard someone got a letter today,"

Shannon said at dinner that evening, her eyes twinkling.

"Who needs pony express to deliver the mail when they have store owners like the Graysons? They tell you everyone else's business too, or just mine?" Brian asked.

"Don't get uppity with my wife. She only wants the best for you. Both of us do," Mitch retorted angrily.

"Sorry Shannon, I didn't mean to sound short," Brian said.

"So, what did she say? Does she sound nice?" Shannon seemed so genuinely interested, Brian felt even worse for biting her head off.

"I don't know Shannon, she didn't say much. Here you can read it," he said, offering her the letter.

"No, I couldn't do that," Shannon said.

"Go on, we all know you're desperate to. I'm giving you permission." Brian handed the note to Shannon with a smile to show he wasn't being nasty.

"Not much of a correspondent, is she?" Shannon said after a moment. "Maybe she's shy. It's hard to write to someone you don't know."

"You managed it well enough," Mitch said. "We exchanged letters for an… ouch. What was that for?"

Brian had to hide a smile as Shannon glared at her husband making it obvious they hadn't had a problem exchanging letters.

"Mitchell Williams, there are some days I believe you were kicked in the head by a mule. What did you have to go and say that for?" Shannon's eyes glowed with temper.

Mitch turned various shades of red before he mumbled, "Sorry. I didn't think."

"Brian, you pay my husband no heed. Everyone is different. I am sure Bridget will be a lovely girl and a wonderful wife."

"Guess we'll find out soon enough," Brian said, praying Shannon was right.

CHAPTER 18

*B*ridget accompanied Lily to Father Nelson's house where she was to meet the man who would supervise the orphan boys.

"Bridget, Lily, come in out of the rain," Father Nelson greeted them, waving his hand to usher them inside. "Awful miserable day, isn't it? You would think you were in Ireland if you closed your eyes and didn't see all the buildings."

Bridget didn't respond to Father Nelson; she was far too nervous. What if the man didn't agree to her traveling with him? Lily squeezed her hand as if trying to give her support. Bridget managed to smile. Mrs. Riordan brought in tea and cakes but didn't acknowledge any of them.

"Don't mind Mrs. Riordan. She still doesn't consider me acceptable company for Father Nelson," Lily whispered in Bridget's ear. She didn't get a chance to respond as the door opened and Father Nelson walked in with another gentleman. He was tall in stature and so thin you would think he would blow away in a strong wind. Bridget guessed he was about thirty years old, although his black clothes might have made him look older. He wiped his feet on the mat as he came into the room.

"Bridget, this is Mr. Carl Watson. He is a committed member of the Outplacement Society as well as a qualified teacher. Mr. Watson, Bridget Collins is doing us a huge favor. She is en route to Riverside Springs and has agreed to fill in for Maud Simmons who has fallen ill."

"I hope Maud recovers quickly. She is a

respected member of our organization." Mr. Watson said, then turned his attention to Bridget.

Bridget's cheeks heated up under the man's scrutiny. She could sense his eyes travel from her boots to the top of her head and back down again. He seemed to be studying her and although it should have made her feel uncomfortable, she found herself blushing at the glimpse of admiration she fancied she saw in his eyes. A second later it was gone, making her think she had imagined it.

She wondered how many times he had made this trip with orphans. He wasn't at all like she'd expected although if anyone asked her what she thought a placement officer would look like, she wouldn't have been able to answer. He looked…sad. That was the word.

"Miss Collins." The man nodded. "We will have our hands full this trip, we have thirty-eight children to place."

"Why don't you take a seat Mr. Watson? Would you prefer tea or coffee? Mrs. Riordan has supplied tea, but she would be happy to make coffee as well," Lily offered, smiling.

"Water is fine, thank you," Mr. Watson said. He pulled at his collar before taking a seat on the very edge of the chair. Bridget tried not to stare at him, but her gaze kept returning to his face. He wasn't the most attractive man she had ever seen but there was something about him. She wondered what he did when he wasn't escorting the orphans. Was he still teaching? His hands, rough and ridged with old scars, were not the hands of a teacher but those of a gardener maybe? But didn't gardeners have mud encrusted fingernails? He was picking at some fluff on his suit. Was he nervous? Surely, he had met Father Nelson and Lily before?

CHAPTER 19

*B*ridget clasped the cup of tea between her hands using the heat to distract her from Mr. Watson.

"I am depending on you to teach Miss Collins and provide her with support, "Father Nelson said. "She may find it rather difficult to break ties with some of the children, in particular her own siblings."

Mr. Watson jumped to his feet. "She is taking her siblings? Absolutely not. I totally forbid it. It will upset the other children."

Bridget was about to argue when Father Nelson intervened.

"Mr. Watson, I think you forget yourself." Father Nelson didn't shout but his tone was enough to get everyone's attention. "Bridget Collins has her reasons for leaving New York. It is not her fault she finds herself in this predicament. I will not tolerate any lack of consideration for her feelings. Is that clear?"

Mr. Watson looked from the priest to Bridget and back again. "Yes, Father," Mr. Watson said. "I apologize. Forgive me please. I get carried away sometimes."

Bridget caught the glance Mr. Watson sent her expecting to see anger but finding pity. She shifted in her seat. She didn't want anyone feeling sorry for her.

"I will make sure Bridget is up to date on everything. She will be ready and willing." Lily glanced at Bridget before turning her attention back to the man. "Bridget is gifted with children. She will be a huge asset to you during this trip, Mr. Watson."

"Father Nelson," Mr. Watson said, ignoring the comment about Bridget. "We must ensure each child has a suitable set of clothes. It is hard enough to find families without the orphans looking like—"

"The poverty-stricken children that they are?" Lily's tone told Bridget she was upset, but the man didn't take any notice of her. His whole focus was on Father Nelson. It was almost as if the women weren't present.

"Mr. Watson, we will do our best to outfit the children properly, but your insistence on white aprons for the girls is going a little far. Especially as the journey on the train is so dirty. How can anyone keep them clean, let alone a child?" Father Nelson asked.

"I know it sounds like I am making unreasonable demands, but I assure you everything we can do for these children, to make them more attractive, is worthwhile," Mr. Wilson said earnestly.

"Is it difficult to find homes for the children?" Bridget's question drew his attention to her. For a second, she saw real pain and the depth of it shocked her. But then it was gone. "We have siblings staying in the sanctuary, Lizzie and Jacob Kelley. They must be kept together."

"The economic depression is making everyone feel rather nervous. Some people who may have been willing to take a child might not believe they can afford to. It is even less likely siblings will be adopted together. And there are others who may take advantage of the situation."

"What do you mean?"

"Mr. Watson, don't be putting Bridget off now before she goes on the trip. Everything will work out just fine in the end." Father Nelson's tone brooked no argument. Bridget saw Mr. Watson open his mouth but then shut it again.

"How does the actual process work, Father?" Bridget asked.

"There are two parts to your group," Father Nelson said. "The first are the little ones from the Foundling Hospital. These children have been specifically asked for."

"So why do they have to travel with us by train if their adoptive parents want them? Why didn't they collect them at the time of adoption?" Bridget asked.

"They haven't yet met them," Mr. Watson explained. "When Father Nelson means is we get various requests for babies. One man wrote and asked for a red-headed boy, he has, I think, seven girls and despairs of ever having a son. He wants a boy to carry on his name."

"He can't just order a child like you would something from a store catalogue." Bridget couldn't hide her disgust. Her comment earned a smile from Mr. Watson but a reprimand from Father Nelson.

"Why not? He is willing to provide a loving home for a baby who could otherwise die," Father Nelson replied, but in a softer tone added, "Bridget, I know it is hard to accept but sometimes, things work for the right reason even though the method leaves a lot to be desired. If people write to us asking for a blond-haired girl, or one with black hair and blue eyes, we do our best to answer their request."

"But what if their ideal baby doesn't grow up to become the child they imagined they would be?" Bridget asked.

Bridget saw Lily glance at Father Nelson, but he seemed unwilling to answer. Mr. Watson stared at the floor.

"These kids need a home," Lily said, her voice shaking. "In an ideal world, they would be adopted by people desperate for children of their own. But we don't live in a world like that. The one we live in means the Foundling Hospital had to put a cradle at their door to try to stop desperate women from leaving new-borns on the cold steps, or in the nearest bin."

"Oh, Lily, what sort of world do we live in?" Bridget asked, trying to stop the tears filling her eyes. She refused to cry in public.

"Shush," Lily said gently. "We do the best we can, one step at a time."

"The rest is in God's hands. You can help

him by preparing the children as best you can on the journey. Talk to them, tell them stories, try to assuage their fears." Father Nelson groaned as he lowered himself back into a chair, having stood up to take another cookie. "Reassure them they can write to us if they are unhappy."

"Write? Most of the children aren't literate and those that are, are older. What about the younger ones? Who protects them?" Bridget couldn't stop herself from asking.

"Bridget, settle down now. We do our best. That is all we can do," Father Nelson replied in a tired tone.

Lily sent her a sweet smile while at the same time shaking her head. Bridget took the hint and stayed quiet.

"I should leave. I have some people to see. Good evening Father Nelson, Mrs. Doherty." Mr. Watson took Bridget's hand as if to shake it but held onto it for seconds longer than necessary. "Try to get a lot of rest before Saturday, Miss Collins. Sleeping on a train is not easy."

And then he was gone. Bridget stared after him until Father Nelson interrupted.

"Bridget, be ready at eight a.m. on Saturday morning," Father Nelson said. "I will collect you then."

"Thank you, Father Nelson." Bridget knew she owed the priest a large debt. He had saved her and her family, but how could he stand behind such a scheme as the orphan train?

CARL WATSON LIMPED out of the room, and out the front door as fast as he could. Scamp jumped as soon as the door opened, wagging his tail as if it had been years since he saw Carl, not less than an hour ago. He sniffed at his hand.

"Sorry, out of luck, old boy. I forgot to bring you a cookie, I left in a hurry."

Why had he? What must Miss Collins think of him rushing off like that? She would think him a frightful bore.

But her questions were those he asked himself continuously? What type of society provided children by order like a shopping catalogue. Miss Collins was correct to wonder what happened when the sought-after baby didn't grow into the much-desired child? He scowled. He knew the answer to that question all too well.

Maud, the lady who usually accompanied him on his travels, never questioned anything. Maud was a nice girl, in fact he felt safe around her. He could talk to her easier than any other woman he had encountered.

Miss Collins on the other hand, had his tongue tied up in knots. Ironic, given she seemed to come from his class,whereas Maud came from one of the wealthier families in New York. Maud's rather forceful mother believed her daughter should do some charity work before settling down to get married. She was well-educated and interesting to talk to, although she lacked backbone. She wasn't particularly interested in the children they placed, not that she would mistreat any, but she didn't fight for them like he believed they deserved.

He sensed Miss Collins was already attached to some of the children they would travel with. Her siblings obviously but also Jacob and Lizzie. He had handled the issue of her taking her siblings on the train badly, but he couldn't bear the hurt and pain she was setting herself up for. Giving up your own family had to be the hardest thing anyone had to do.

He threw a stick for Scamp to race after ignoring the glares from the people around him. He had to distract himself from that line of thinking.

Why couldn't Maud be coming this time? She was a known quantity. She didn't ask any questions and she didn't form any emotional attachments with the children. Most of all, she didn't cause his heart to beat faster or his collar to feel like it was strangling him. He couldn't remember when a woman had so appealed to him. Especially one as strong-willed and opinionated as Miss Collins seemed to be. He wondered what her story was?

Her clothes, while flattering, weren't quite right. Not that she would dress like Maud in any event. One dress Maud wore could feed a whole train of starving orphans for the month. Maud wouldn't be caught dead wearing a long blue skirt that didn't quite reach the floor. He had glimpsed a pair of rather fetching ankles. Oh, what was he doing thinking about Miss Collins? They had to work together for the next two months or however long it took to find homes for all the children.

The children were his priority not anything else. He limped faster as if by putting physical distance between him and the young lady with the brown curls escaping from her bun would remove her from his mind.

CHAPTER 20

*L*ily hailed a cab and they rode back to the sanctuary in silence. Bridget wanted to ask Lily more, but the look on the other woman's face stopped her. She had never seen Lily look so sad and it unsettled her.

"Bridget, you will need to read these," Lily said, handing her a small pile of papers. "They are the rules regarding the children. I expect Mr. Watson has them memorized, so you might want to learn them as well."

"Thanks, Lily. Do you know if there will be

anyone else to help with the babies? I think Father Nelson mentioned there might be more than one."

"I think you have four going on this trip," Lily said. "The older girls will help you. It seems the charity doesn't have the money to employ more adults to help."

"Or it's not their priority," Bridget said.

"I understand you are disappointed and possibly quite shocked, but they do the best they can. The economy is struggling, and quite a few of the richer benefactors are finding themselves having to reduce their spending."

"Sorry, Lily. I just get so upset thinking of those children. It's one thing to be orphaned but another to be given up because your mother cannot afford to keep you. Can you imagine how hard it would be for anyone to do...Oh Lily, please don't cry. I didn't mean to upset you."

"I know Bridget. It's not really you. It's just...well this morning I found out I am not with child. I thought maybe this time I would be. I've tried for so long." Lily put her head in her hands and wept. Bridget stood for a moment before moving over to her new friend and putting her arms around her. Lily's sobs grew louder. "Four years we have been wed and still no sign of a baby. I think God is angry with me for my past sins."

"Lily, no. Don't think like that. He couldn't possibly be angry with you, not when you do so much good for others," Bridget assured her. "He isn't like that anyway. We cannot believe in a God who is vindictive. Likely it isn't the right time for you and your husband. You will have a baby when He believes you are ready."

"Bridget, how I wish I believed that. But I think there may be a reason for why I never fell pregnant. After all those years of abuse. I…oh, what does it matter. Crying won't cure anything."

"No," Bridget agreed. "But I always feel better after a good cry. You are so brave and strong all the time. You don't have to be like that. You have real friends who care about you. Let them help you."

"I shall miss you, Bridget. Even though we have only known each other these few short weeks."

"Maybe I can come back to New York to see you sometime, or you can come visit me in Wyoming. I heard it's beautiful," Bridget said.

"Thank you," Lily said, dabbing at her eyes with a handkerchief. "I'd best get my face sorted out, or Mrs. Wilson will send me home to bed. Bridget, go find your family and take some time with them. Bring Kathleen too. You need to explain what is happening."

"Thank you, Lily."

"I know I wouldn't relish a journey with Mr. Watson, but please try to see it as a means to an end. He will be busy looking after the children under his care, so hopefully he won't have much time to annoy you," Lily said.

"Lily, I can't ever repay all you have done for me. For us."

"Yes, you can," Lily said. "All I ask is that

you help someone less fortunate. If everyone helps someone who then helps someone the world would be in a better place than it is now. Small steps will lead to big actions. At least that is what Charlie, my husband, keeps telling me."

Bridget gave Lily a hug, then, before she started crying herself, left to go spend time with her family. After Saturday who knew when she would see Kathleen and Maura again, if ever.

But Bridget didn't go straight back to her room. Instead, she went to find Mrs. Wilson and told her Lily was upset but not the reason.

"Thank you, Bridget. I will go to her now. You have a lovely heart young lady. Try never to let that go."

Bridget didn't reply. Mrs. Wilson had already walked away.

BRIDGET WAS ABOUT to go into the room she

shared with her sisters when Bella called to her. The younger girl seemed quite agitated and clearly wanted to speak to Bridget in private. She followed Bella into the work room which, since it was nighttime, was empty.

"What's wrong, Bella?"

"I heard you are going on the orphan train. Don't let them take Annie or Liam away from you. But especially Annie."

"I won't," Bridget tried to reassure the girl, while wondering how news had traveled so fast.

"I mean it, Bridget. You have no idea what they do to orphans," Bella spoke, the whole time looking around her as if afraid someone would hear.

"Bella, sit here and tell me why you are so scared. You know Lily would never do anything to hurt you. Or anyone else here. Has someone threatened you?"

Taking a deep breath, Bella sat, but then immediately stood up again. Bridget drew her gently into the seat beside her. She put her arm around the younger girl's shoulders.

"Tell me, Bella. I promise to help if I can."

Bella stood. "I got to show you something." She slipped the top of her dress from her shoulders to show Bridget her back. Bridget gasped at the ugly scars crisscrossing the girl's shoulder blades.

"Bella, who did that to you? Oh, you poor girl." Standing, Bridget covered the girl's back and hugged her close.

"The woman who took me from the orphan train," Bella said. "I don't know what she wanted. Everything I did was wrong, and she used to hit me with her rawhide whip. I close my eyes, and I can still hear the sound of the leather screaming through the air."

"Oh Bella. I am so sorry," Bridget said. "But perhaps you were just unlucky."

"Lots of orphans on the trains be unlucky. I tried to run away but they kept sending me back. Then her husband, he, he…" The girl shuddered, leaving Bridget to guess what had happened. Her grip on the girl tightened.

"Bridget, you can't give Annie to a family like that. She is so pretty. She looks like a little angel. You got to promise you won't."

Bridget held Bella while she sobbed. The poor girl whom she had dismissed as being hard as nails, appeared to care more about Annie than Maura did.

"I promise you, Bella. I won't do it. You are safe now, you know that, right?"

Bella didn't answer.

"I saw you put something in your pocket the other day," Bridget said. "I didn't want to ask you what it was."

"It was just a dream is all."

"What dreams, Bella? You can tell me."

Bella looked uncertain but then she put her hand in her pocket and took out a dog-eared piece of paper. She handed it to Bridget. It was an ad from a man looking for a wife.

"Bella, you are too young to get married," Bridget said.

"I know, but I could lie about my age. If I were married, I wouldn't be an orphan no more."

"Oh, Bella, this is not the way. You don't know anything about this man. He may mistreat you. You cannot trust a stranger."

"It was just a dream. Who'd want me anyway?"

Bridget stroked the younger girl's hair back from her eyes. "Someone would be lucky to marry you, Bella, when you are a little older. You have a big heart, although you hide it well. Why don't you tell Lily about this man?"

"She hates me."

"Lily?" Bridget asked, surprised. "No, she doesn't. Lily couldn't hate anyone. You sometimes look quite scary, so maybe she doesn't see you as I do. But talk to her, Bella. She can help. I know she can."

Bella stared at the ground, her expression reminding Bridget of Annie when she was told to go to bed early.

"Please, Bella. You trusted me with your

secret, now why don't you trust what I am telling you is right."

Bella looked her in the eye. "I don't trust no one."

"No, and I can't blame you for that," Bridget said. "But until you learn to trust yourself and those around you, you will never be happy."

Bella shrugged her shoulders, taking the newspaper copy and put it back in her pocket.

"I liked you. I hope you get to be happy." Then, after one fierce hug, she was gone.

EXHAUSTED, Bridget lay beside Kathleen, but sleep eluded her. Every time she closed her eyes, she saw Mr. Wilson. He intrigued her. At first, she had thought him to be cold, formal, and more interested in doing things by the book rather than in the interests of the children. But she sensed there was more to him than what she had seen. For instance, the expressions on his face when Father Nelson was describing the baby outplacement service suggested he didn't share Father Nelson's belief it was a good solution. But then his insistence on white aprons for all the girls was taking things a bit far wasn't it? There were more important things in life.

CHAPTER 21

Saturday morning came all too quickly. Her eyes red, Kathleen had elected to say goodbye at the sanctuary, saying she would embarrass the Collins name if she were to travel to the train station. Maura hadn't said a word and didn't make an effort, not even to hug Liam or Annie.

"Write to me Bridget, never forget me," Kathleen begged.

"Forget you? Never," Bridget promised. "You will always have a piece of my heart."

"Look after Bridget and Annie, Liam. You are the man of the family now," Kathleen said.

"I am? I thought Shane and Michael were going on the train as well," Liam said.

"They are, darling, but not this one. Now say goodbye to Kathleen. We can't be late," Bridget replied.

Bridget could only imagine how Mr. Carl Watson would react if they were not on time. She didn't want to get into his bad books any further, although, to be honest, she hoped they had very little to do with one another on the journey.

They were to meet the children at the station. Thankfully, Lily had agreed to come to say goodbye as had Father Nelson. Looking ahead, she spotted Mr. Watson standing with some children and a dog. It looked like one of the many strays that roamed the railway. She hoped the children wouldn't be frightened of it. Why wasn't Mr. Watson making it go away? Lily's voice distracted her.

"Please write to me, Bridget, you have become a firm favorite in your short time here."

"I will, Lily. Thank you for everything. Please look after Kathleen. I know you will, but she is so upset."

"I will, don't worry," Lily reassured her.

Then Lily hugged her close before hugging Annie and Liam. Annie was clinging to Bridget as if she would never let her go. Liam was trying to be a man but the look in his eyes told Bridget he was just as terrified as Annie.

"We will be fine," Bridget promised as she bent down, pretending to tie Liam's shoelace. "I won't let anyone take you two. We are going to stick together."

"You swear?" he asked.

"I promise," Bridget gently corrected her little brother.

"Bridget never breaks promises. She isn't like Maura," Liam whispered to Annie putting his arm around the little girl's shoulders. Bridget had to turn away, so he wouldn't know she had heard.

"Please give my regards to Reverend Franklin," Father Nelson said. "Tell him I look forward to our next game of chess."

"I didn't know you saw him regularly, Father Nelson. Does that mean you come out to Riverside Springs sometimes?" Bridget asked, hope making her voice squeak.

"Sadly, no," he answered. "The last game of chess we played was about twenty years ago. Around the time he transferred out of New York. I miss him."

"I will tell him, Father. Thank you for everything you did for my family."

"May God look after you and your family. Trust him, Bridget. You may not always understand why things happen, but there is always a reason."

"Yes, Father," Bridget replied more or less automatically. If there was a reason her lovely family had to split up, she really couldn't see it. But now was not the time to argue with the old man.

"Miss Collins, if you are quite ready," Mr. Watson prompted her.

Bridget looked up at the cold tone but was surprised to see a flicker of something in the man's eyes. Pity? Understanding? Then it was gone, to be replaced by what she was going to call his teacher's face. The stray dog was by his feet, but he didn't seem to notice although he could have easily hit it with his cane. What had happened to his leg? He was speaking, and she hadn't been paying attention.

"Miss Collins, we need to get the children settled," he went on. "I have divided them up into girls and boys. This young man will have to come with me."

"No," Liam said. "I ain't leaving my sisters."

"Liam, 'ain't' isn't a word we use," Bridget told him. Then to Mr. Watson, "I apologize for my brother, Mr. Watson. He wants to stay with us. I will look after him."

"But I must insist," Mr. Watson answered in a tone that made the dog sit. She would have laughed but for the fact he seemed to be serious.

"You can insist all you like. He stays with me. As do Lizzie and Jacob." Bridget didn't wait to see his reaction but shepherded her family onto the train. She made sure they were seated together before turning her attention to the girls in her charge. Tears filled her eyes as almost twenty faces stared back at her, some younger than Annie. These children were in her care for the next few weeks. She greeted each and every one of them.

"Miss, can I sit with my sister?" one of the girls said to her. "She's only two and needs me."

"Of course, you can, love," Bridget said.

"But the man said…"

Bridget gripped her hands so tightly, her fingernails clawed into her skin. "He made a mistake. You go on and sit with your sister. In fact, all siblings please take a seat together, the older ones will move to sit beside the younger ones."

Bridget waited until she had six sets of sisters seated together. Then she looked at her remaining group and quickly rearranged them so there were older girls matched with younger ones.

"We are going to travel in pairs. I don't want to lose anyone, so each of you are going to be responsible for the younger child sitting next to you. Any questions?"

"No, ma'am," came the chorus.

"You can call me Bridget, not ma'am, if you prefer."

"They will call you ma'am, Miss Collins," Mr. Watson said, walking up behind her. "You are not their friend but their supervisor. Now come with me, we need to collect the babies." Mr. Watson looked at the older girls for a moment before pointing to three of them. "You, you and you, please come with me to help."

Bridget followed Mr. Watson from the train after telling Liam to remain in his seat with Annie. She bit back her anger at the way he had addressed the girls, surely, he could have made an effort to learn their names. The dog followed him once more.

"What are you going to do about the dog?" she asked.

"What do you mean, do?'

"Maybe he is hungry. He seems to be following you?"

"He's always hungry. Don't fall for his tricks. He is good at gathering sympathy aren't you, Scamp?"

To his amazement, Miss Collins actually caressed the scraggly looking mutt. The dog's tail wagged so fast it was a wonder it didn't fall off.

"You know him?"

"Scamp is my best friend, Miss Collins. Anywhere I go, he comes too. Isn't that right fella?"

The dog woofed as in agreement.

"But he's a dog," she said, realizing she was stating the obvious.

A pair of twinkling eyes looked back at her as if he was laughing.

"I mean he could be dangerous to the children." She tried to justify her comment, but it only seemed to amuse him more.

"Scamp would never hurt a child." He rubbed the dog's head before staring at her. "Miss Collins, he won't touch anyone unless I tell him to. The dog stays. I trust him more than I trust most humans. Dog's don't lie."

She stared at the dog for a couple of seconds, thinking he might be a good distraction for the children.

"We have four babies on this journey. The older girls will help you," he told her.

The abrupt change of subject caught her off guard and she was silent for a couple of seconds.

"I take it by your silence you agree?"

"You could always take the baby boys," she suggested. Bridget knew she shouldn't irritate him, but she couldn't help herself. "You know, seeing as you have separated everyone including siblings."

"I did what I was told," he said. "Perhaps you should try following suit."

Bridget stared at him for a couple of seconds before she replied, in a tone she usually reserved for Annie and Liam when they were misbehaving. "I will take the babies as they need cuddles and hugs as well as feeding and changing. I suggest, in fact, I insist you go back on that train and rearrange the seating to allow siblings to sit together. This may be the last time those children see their families. Who are you to stop them from spending time together?"

He came to a standstill, stopped a minute, and then turned to face her. She couldn't read the expression on his face. It seemed to be a mixture of surprise and irritation.

"Who am I?" he asked. "I would better ask who do you think you are? I am in charge here, Miss Collins, and if you don't like it, you better get used to it. It is my role to make sure these children are placed, and we do not have to bring them back to New York. Is that clear?"

"No, it isn't," she said, standing firm.

"Pardon? Are you feebleminded? If we do not place the children with families, we will have to bring them back to live in New York."

"I understand that much," Bridget said. "What you don't understand is your role is not to place these children like one would place parcels on a goods train. Our job on this train is to ensure these children go to loving homes where possible. At the very least they go to homes whose occupants will provide them with food, care, and schooling. That is your role, Mr. Watson. And you best get used to it."

She swept past him, not waiting for a reply. If he argued back with her, she could very well push him under the train. Well, she wouldn't really, although she would love to. She muttered a prayer asking for forgiveness for her lack of patience.

CHAPTER 22

She walked off to greet the representative from the foundling hospital, thankful the nun hadn't heard her exchange with Mr. Watson.

"My name is Bridget Collins, Sister. Father Nelson asked me to help on this trip as the usual lady, Maud, is ill."

"Oh, dear me, you don't look old enough to care for four babies," the nun said, eyeing her skeptically.

What age did the nun think she was? She had been caring for little kids since she was practically no more than one herself. It was the way in the tenements.

"I am nineteen, Sister, and have plenty of practice. Father Nelson told me every baby had a note with it, so we know which family to give the child to," Bridget said.

"Yes, they do," the nun confirmed. "This dear little one is Martha, this one is David, the far one is Patrick, and the one in the pram still asleep is Kathleen. She has a touch of an upset stomach so needs regular water. Martha likes her…"

"That's enough, Sister John Bosco," another, older nun spoke up. "The girl will take over now. It's time to get back to the Convent. We have wasted too much time here already."

Bridget couldn't believe the older nun's attitude. Where was her heart? She opened her mouth to object, but the younger nun shook her head.

CARL WATSON HAD WATCHED the expressions cross Miss Collin's face before she walked off. She was like an open book, so easy to read. Well, she would learn not to wear her heart on her sleeve. If she didn't, she would end up with a broken heart. Like his. He kept watching, scratching Scamp's head right behind his ear, until she reached the nun. He was about to turn away when he spotted Sister Constance. That was one woman who should never be allowed anywhere near a child. He moved quickly in order to help Miss Collins when Sister Constance started throwing her weight around as she was apt to do.

As he had suspected, she was bullying Sister John Bosco, another lady who wore her heart on her sleeve. If he had a dollar for every time he had seen the younger nun show kindness to a child, he would be a wealthy man. He moved quickly to remove Sister Constance and allow the younger nun say goodbye to the babies. He sensed Miss Collins would see his actions for what they were, so he formed a mask over his face. It wouldn't do for her to believe he had feelings. Women considered men like that to be weak. That lesson he had learned the hard way.

"Good morning, Sister Constance, John Bosco," Mr. Watson said, walking over to them. "I see you have met my assistant for the trip. Sister Constance, if you wish to return to your cab, be my guest. But Sister John Bosco will provide details on each child to Miss Collins and the girls."

Mr. Watson nodded to Sister John Bosco and then to Bridget who was staring at him with her mouth open, before he turned back in the direction of the train.

BRIDGET NEARLY FELL OVER. He had a heart after all. He was giving the younger nun a chance to make sure each of her charges was cared for properly. She looked to his face, but his head was turned away, so she couldn't see his expression.

"As I was saying, Martha seems to sense change and it unsettles her. She likes this blanket, left with her by her mother." The nun whispered the last words, her anxious gaze darting toward the other nun.

"Thank you, Sister, I will see it stays with her," Bridget assured her.

"David is a wee pet, would sleep forever if you don't wake him to be fed. Patrick, well, some would say he is the troublemaker, but I think he just needs the most love."

Bridget took each baby carefully as the Nun passed them over but only after she had hugged each one close. She gave each of the three oldest girls a baby to take onto the train. She thought Sister John Bosco would make a natural mother and wondered what had made her become a nun. With tears in her eyes, the young nun hurried away as soon as the last baby was in Bridget's arms.

Mr. Watson was waiting at the car door as she made her way back.

"Thank you for intervening back there," Bridget said as nicely as she could.

"I only did what was best for our trip. Now if you could take your place please, the train is ready to depart."

Bridget bit her lip rather than respond. She had tried being nice and he threw it back in her face. The man would try the patience of Job.

CHAPTER 23

Carl turned to attend to the luggage, then the conductor approached him, a look of disgust on his face. Scamp snarled at the uniformed man making Carl put his hand on the dog's head. It wouldn't do for the dog to be thrown off.

"Mr. Watson, you going to keep this rabble under control? I have a train full of real people who do not want their journey to be—"

"Rabble?" Carl interrupted, using his coldest tone to good effect as the bluster drained out of the conductor. Scamp growled.

"The children, I mean," the man corrected himself.

"The children will behave," Carl said. "Now why don't you go and do your job and let me get on with mine."

The man walked off as Carl stared after him. People like the conductor were part of the problem with the world today. Those who would look at such a miserable bunch of misfit, unwanted children and instead of seeing all they needed was love, kindness, and a firm hand, would assume they were thieves and goodness knows what else in the making. He wished he hadn't agreed to do this role again. It was thankless as well as heartbreaking. He knew, despite his best efforts, that these orphans, or at least the older ones, were as likely to get adopted into loving families as he was to fall in love and have a family of his own.

Still it wasn't going to help anyone if he went soft now. The children needed to be prepared for the life ahead of them. The worst thing he could do was give them the impression that kindness and love were waiting for them. As he worked through the supplies, making sure each child got their allocation, his mind kept straying to Bridget Collins. Although this was her first trip with the outplacement society, she had risen to the challenge of the role admirably.

She had such a big heart, making sure every child felt important. They weren't just orphans to her but real people. She would try her best to find them good homes. He would have to make sure she wasn't too idealistic as they couldn't afford to return all thirty plus children back to New York. The grim reality was, that the New York tenements offered almost certain death in the future for these children. At least with foster families they stood a chance. Some would meet wonderful, caring families who would treat them like their own. Others would meet individuals who would raise them to be hard workers and respectful of themselves and others. The minority, or so he hoped, would end up with people who would mistreat them.

At best, all he could do was to hopefully protect the children from the worst of the abuse. No child would end up in a family like the one that had adopted him.

CHAPTER 24

*B*ridget scrutinized the children. Thankfully, Mr. Watson had given in to her request to have siblings sit together. It was actually easier to handle a mixed group of children than it would be to leave the boys together to rile each other on.

She walked down the car loosening the leather straps on the windows to encourage more air. She didn't want any child falling out, so she encouraged the older, or more responsible children, to sit by the windows. When the train started moving, the buildings whizzed by, exciting the children. Then they left the buildings of New York behind and the scenery gradually became greener with open fields rather than grey tenements.

"Look there's cows. My ma used to milk cows back in Ireland," one of the younger children commented.

"Milk comes from the horse and cart on the street, stupid. Not from an animal," a slightly older boy replied.

"You're stupid. The cow gives us the milk don't they, Miss Collins?"

Bridget listened to them chattering, full of curiosity. For most of them it was the first time they had seen wide-open spaces, never mind cows and sheep. One of the younger girls pulled on her sleeve, her expression suggesting she was about to cry.

"Yes, Lizzie?" Bridget asked.

"Where have all the people gone? You said we would find families."

"We have to reach a town first. Come here." Bridget moved baby Martha to her other arm to let Lizzie sit on her knee. Then she pointed at the homesteads in the distance. "See those are houses, the people who live in them probably own the land and the animals you see."

"They must be rich. Imagine having all that space to call your own." Lizzie gazed in wonder at the view, all the while sucking her thumb. Bridget prayed the little one would find a family to give her the stability she craved. She had grown to love the little girl and also to admire her brother Jacob. But it would be difficult to place her in a home with Jacob.

She looked up to see Jacob watching her with Lizzie, his expression suggesting he was anticipating trouble. Despite living in the sanctuary with them for a few weeks, he didn't seem to trust her. His hard stare only served to highlight the jagged scar on his face. She could imagine people being scared if they met him on a street. They may even cross the road to avoid him.

They wouldn't give him a chance, get to

know the loving, sensitive boy hiding behind the scar. His hard stare was a defense, a way of protecting himself from the dangers on the streets, but those who had never had to deal with the underworld of New York may not understand.

He was so protective of his little sister that they were inseparable. Lily had given Jacob a bed in with the other boys, but he'd insisted on sleeping on the floor beside Lizzie's bed.

"You look perplexed, Miss Collins."

Startled, she looked up at Mr. Watson. She hadn't noticed him walking toward her, nor heard Scamp panting as he came to rest at her feet. She had been miles away.

"I was just thinking that's all," she said.

"About?"

"The lives the children have led to date and the mark it has made on them. Some, like Sally's injury, are more visible than others."

He followed her gaze toward Jacob and nodded. "That young boy has seen more in his short lifetime than most adults."

"Do you know how his face got so scarred?" she asked, curiosity getting the better of her as to how much he knew about the orphans in his care.

He shook his head.

"His father hit him."

At his harsh intake of breath, she explained that Jacob and Lizzie were the only siblings to survive from a family of eight. Their mother and baby brother Ben had died recently, the other siblings had died in various accidents over the years.

"I cannot understand why he wasn't locked up?" she asked as if Mr. Watson would be able to enlighten her. "The children should have been taken away from him."

"Why are we about to escort thirty-eight children across America to find them new homes? If you are going to work for the Out-placement Society, you have to accept that bad things happen. We don't live in a fair or just world."

Bridget didn't reply. What could she say?

He sounded so jaded for someone so young. Now she sat beside him, she knew he was likely in his mid-twenties and not thirties as she had originally thought. She wanted to ask him why he was so detached when he appeared to care for the children, but she couldn't find the words.

CHAPTER 25

*C*arl tried his best to avoid spending time with Jacob and Lizzie but no matter what he tried, Lizzie kept seeking him out. Seeing the love they had for each other was too painful a reminder. He didn't rate their chances of being adopted together very highly and he knew from experience the pain that would cause. He was sitting with Scamp one afternoon while the train engineers topped up on water and coal when Lizzie came over to sit by him.

"How old is Scamp?" Lizzie asked as she

patted the dog who rolled over, so she could scratch his tummy. "I'd love a puppy, but my Pa never liked dogs."

"I am not sure, but I guess about five years."

"Where did you find him?" Lizzie asked, without looking away from the dog.

"He found me. We were in a town, placing some children in new homes, and he kept trailing after us." Carl tried to keep his tone light but remembering the state of the dog when they'd first met always made him angry. Scamp had been as thin as a weed and dirtier than any animal he had ever seen. His body bore signs of abuse as well. A group of boys had been tormenting the poor animal with sticks and he had intervened. The dog hadn't left his side since.

"I like him. He doesn't look like a kind dog, but he is."

"You can't judge people or animals by how they look, Lizzie. It's what's inside their hearts that matters. Scamp won't win any beauty prizes, but he has a heart the size of the ocean." Carl looked up to catch Miss Collins smiling at him. He clenched his jaw. He didn't want her looking at him the way she was, as if he was someone to be admired. He knew better.

"That's like Jacob. I know you don't like him, but he is the best brother ever."

"I like Jacob, Lizzie. Why would you think I don't?" Even as he asked the question, Carl knew the answer. Adults didn't give children enough credit. They picked up on signs most adults missed.

"'Cause you never speak to him. When he comes near you, you walk away. You do that with me too. Why don't you like us, Mr. Watson?"

Carl looked into her piercing blue eyes but instead of Lizzie he saw Hope, his sister who'd disappeared all those years ago.

"I like you both just fine," he said gruffly.

"Why don't you tell us stories like you do with the others? I thought it was because of Jacob's face, but you said it didn't matter what a person looked like."

Carl stuttered, not knowing how to explain his behavior without scaring her. She was completely innocent of what the future could hold for her and her brother. She stared at him waiting for his reply.

"Lizzie, don't be asking questions. Mr. Watson has his reasons."

Carl looked at the boy, shame making his collar feel tight. He had hurt these two children by making them believe he didn't care. He did, if he was honest he cared too much. He had warned Miss Collins not to get personally involved yet he was guilty of doing that. But he couldn't let them believe he disliked them. That wasn't fair.

"Jacob, Lizzie, I do like you. Both of you. It's just you remind me of some people I knew once, and those memories are rather painful. Now why don't we go back and join the others?"

"Who?" Lizzie said, staring up at him, her

thumb in her mouth and the other still rubbing Scamp's stomach.

"What?" he replied.

"Who were those people?"

"Lizzie, will you quit asking questions. Mr. Watson doesn't need to explain himself." Jacob threw a glance at Carl and he saw the curiosity and was it fear, lurking in the boy's eyes.

"My sister and brother. Now come on children, we have to get things packed up and back onto the train. Jacob, can you take care of Lizzie while I check on the other children?" He didn't wait for an answer but limped quickly toward a group of children playing chase.

Why did he continue taking children on the orphan trains? It was madness, especially as each journey became more painful than the last. Scamp whimpered as if reading his thoughts. It amazed him how the dog tuned into his feelings.

"Wish you could talk to me. Would you tell me to go find another job? One that didn't involve children."

The dog didn't bark but stared at him, head tilted sideways as if asking him could he live with himself if he sat in comfort in New York while these trains still ran, carrying their precious cargo? At least if he were present, he might be able to ensure the children didn't go to unsafe places. There was a huge difference between a place where they would be worked hard and one like he and Tim had ended up in. Tim. He'd failed his brother. He couldn't afford to fail any other child.

The train's whistle announced it was time to rejoin the others. "Come on Scamp, we can't let them leave without us." But when he looked down, Scamp was gone. Carl searched for the animal but couldn't see him until he saw a black head poking out of the train window. Scamp was sitting on Miss Collin's knee. Ungrateful hound – what was he doing sitting with someone else?

CHAPTER 26

*B*ridget tickled the dog behind his ear, but her mind was elsewhere. She couldn't help wondering about Carl Watson and his family. She hadn't meant to listen in on his conversation with Lizzie and Jacob. The children reminded him of his own family. She'd assumed he was an only child as he hadn't mentioned any siblings. But then he hadn't said anything about himself. All she knew was what Father Nelson had told her, he was a teacher having been in the seminary for a few years.

"That's where you got to." His voice sounded gruff. "Down Scamp. I apologize Miss Collins, I hope he didn't get your skirt muddy."

"I encouraged him. I love animals. He's a good dog aren't you boy?"

Scamp obviously agreed if the wagging of his tail was anything to go by.

"Why don't you take a seat too Mr. Watson, you look tired." She glanced up at him. "Are you in pain? You seem to be rather pale if you don't mind me saying?"

He sat, his hand caressing his knee. "Thank you, Miss Collins. My leg is acting up. I may have overdone the walking."

"Did you have an accident?" Bridget wished she could take the words back as soon as they left her mouth. He gritted his teeth in response, his lips tightening into a thin line. "Forgive me, I shouldn't have asked. It's none of my business."

"I fell out of a wagon when I was younger. My leg got caught. I have limped ever since."

"I'm sorry, that must have been very painful."

He glanced at her and for a second she thought he was going to say something, but he didn't. The moment passed.

They sat in silence, the only sound being Scamp who seemed to be laughing in his sleep.

"At least he is happy," Bridget said, smiling at the dog.

"What would it take to make you happy, Miss Collins?"

She looked up quickly to check if he was being sarcastic, but he seemed to be genuinely asking.

"If I could find nice homes for all these children, it would help."

"We do our best, that's all we can do."

She opened her mouth to ask was it? But something stopped her. When he didn't say anything else, she looked at his face to find he had fallen asleep. The poor man was exhausted. She took a rug one of the children had been using but had left on the seat and put it over him. He didn't move.

She took the liberty of examining him as he slept. He looked younger now his face wasn't screwed up in disapproval. But perhaps he had been in pain and she had assumed it was something else. Scamp shuffled nearer to Mr. Watson, his head lying on the man's lap. The dog clearly adored his owner and they said animals were a good judge of character. What she had taken to be coldness and indifference appeared to be a mask hiding a great deal of pain, not all of it physical.

"Miss Collins, can you come? Two of the boys are fighting and it's upsetting the younger girls."

"Yes, Sarah. Coming."

With a last look at Mr. Watson, she walked toward the opposite end of the car where the fight was escalating.

CHAPTER 27

Their last day as a group finally arrived. The next town would host the first meeting with families who had contacted the Outplacement Society. Mr. Watson addressed the group while Bridget sat in the middle of them, two babies on her lap and young girls cuddled to either side of her.

"Tomorrow, we will meet our first group of prospective families. When we arrive at the town, I will take you to the hotel we will be staying in. Miss Collins will take the girls and I the boys. All children will change into these fresh clothes first thing in the morning. When you are dressed, please help the younger ones. Girls, I have lovely white aprons for you to put on over your dresses."

Bridget saw him glance at her when he made this comment, but she decided to ignore it. These children needed her. The fear on their faces, especially on those of the boys who struggled to mask it behind indifferent or sullen expressions, hit her hard. She had ignored the warnings to keep her distance and not get involved on a personal basis. The majority of these children had been deprived of love for far too long and what little she could give them, she was happy to provide.

"Come on children, let's say a prayer we all find nice homes," she said before they settled down on, or in some cases, under, the hard benches in an effort to sleep.

"Are you being adopted too, Miss Collins?" one of the boys asked her.

"Not quite, Jacob but I won't be returning to New York. I am to be married at the end of our trip. I hope my new husband and home are nice."

She looked to the ground but sensed Mr. Watson's eyes on her. When she met his gaze, she saw surprise and something else…could it be disappointment? Hadn't he been told about her circumstances? By the look on his face, he hadn't.

"So, who wants to lead us in the prayer?" Bridget asked.

Sandra, a ten-year-old, put up her hand. "I pray for a ma as nice as the one who left me."

"She wasn't that nice if she left, was she?"

"Peter, apologize to Sandra, that remark wasn't kind," Bridget scolded.

"She didn't have a choice. She died," retorted Sandra, with tears falling down her face.

"Come on children," Bridget quickly intervened. "This isn't helping. Let's all pray. Dear Lord, please find me a family who loves and treats me well. Thank you."

The children bowed their heads, but she caught Mr. Watson's gaze on her again. This time his expression was one of rebuke. Why was he against her praying?

She would ask him, but first, she had to get the children settled for the evening.

"Bridget, do you promise they won't take us?" her brother asked.

"Liam, I promise. Tomorrow you just do as I say, and we will be fine. Nobody is going to split up my family," she said.

"I love you Bridget," Liam said.

"I love you too, darling," she whispered back, kissing him and Annie on the head. Nothing and nobody would make her let these children go. They were a family and that was the way they would stay.

CHAPTER 28

*B*ridget wanted to talk to Carl again. Maybe he would share his story if she made more of an effort to get to know him. He was sitting at the far end of the passenger car, reading a newspaper. She walked up to him, but he didn't acknowledge her presence. She didn't know if he was ignoring her or hadn't seen her.

"Please, excuse me, Mr. Watson, but I was wondering if you could explain the process to me. For when we reach our first town? I have never been at a child..." She was about to say "auction" but that wasn't right, so she let her sentence hang in midair.

"The process? It is quite simple really. We get the children to look the best they can. This is why I insisted on white aprons. You may believe I was just being fussy, but I want to do all I can to get these children placed in homes. Their appearance does make a difference. They will be lined up in ages, oldest down to toddler. The families who signed up and expressed interest will be invited to pick their child and then the next family and so on. This will continue until we run out of children or willing families, whichever happens first."

Bridget had to fight back tears. How could he dismiss the placement of a child in a new family in a strange town so easily? With effort, she composed herself before asking, "What about siblings? Surely we can ask that they stay together?"

"We can ask, but few can afford to adopt two children," he explained. "Those that do adopt more than one tend to adopt boys to work on their farms."

"But what if a sibling is placed at this next town and the other is left?" she asked, afraid to know the answer.

"That child will travel with us until we reach the next destination. He or she will continue until they are placed, or they return to New York."

Bridget stared at him for a couple of seconds, hoping to see some reaction to what he had just said but he might as well be reading Greek from a foreign paper. Surely, he had to care. At least a little bit.

"You mean they may never see each other again? That's inhumane." She tried to keep a lid on her temper.

"Is it? Is offering to bring them both back to New York to the tenements where their lives will be cut short due to illness, abuse or…"

All attempts at restraint fled. "Stop it. Surely you cannot be as heartless as you pretend. These children have nobody. They need someone to fight on their behalf."

"In some towns the people who find the families do a great job. They find those who have good hearts and are willing to offer a child a proper home. At the very least they find people who will treat the child well even if they are only looking for workers."

"What do you mean workers?" Bridget couldn't help the accusing note in her voice. Given the stories the girls at the sanctuary had told her, especially Bella's, she knew more than she ever wanted to know.

"Nobody explained this to you, did they?" Mr. Watson asked, in a much gentler tone.

Bridget shook her head. They had but she sensed he was going to give her additional details.

"Farmers are having a difficult time of things at the moment. They need workers for the land but cannot afford to pay the wages grown men would command. So instead they turn to the children." Mr. Watson ignored her gasp of horror and continued. "In return for a promise to school the children in the winter months, provide them with shelter and food, they indenture a boy until he is twenty-one years old. When he reaches that age, he is free to leave. The family must provide him with a new suit and some wages at that time."

"Free to leave? You mean he is their property?"

"Not exactly. If the circumstances prove unsatisfactory the boy can write to the agency and one of our staff will investigate. He can then be removed if his situation is as bad as he alleges."

"But most of the older boys cannot read or write properly. They weren't given enough schooling. How are they supposed to contact anyone?"

"I do not make the rules, Miss Collins. The agency is supposed to inspect the placements within a year of the child being placed."

"I can guess from what you are not saying, this doesn't happen a lot."

She saw the despair in his eyes before he looked away. He did care more than he showed. She wondered why he fought so hard to put on such a cold front. It didn't help the children or her.

"You don't believe they are doing the best they can, do you?" she asked him, wanting to force him to admit the truth.

"America is a large country and the agency's resources are stretched. There isn't the time or the money to always do the right thing."

"But that's no excuse. These are children. Innocent children," Bridget pleaded.

"I am aware of that Miss Collins."

His tone stopped her mid-tirade. Something told her she was pushing him too far. Not only did he understand more than she realized, he was as disgusted by what he described as much as she was. Although, looking at him, at his closed inscrutable expression, she wondered if that was just her imagination.

"What of the girls? How do we prevent

them from becoming…" Her cheeks flamed but she had to continue, "workers?"

She knew by his expression he knew what she meant.

"We try to make sure they are being adopted for the right reasons. The girls are expected to help out in the house or on the farm. If you are suspicious that is not the reason behind the choice, you must speak up. In private though, Miss Collins. You won't do anyone any good by throwing a fit of temper in front of a whole town. Remember this is only one group of children. There are hundreds, if not thousands, more to be placed."

She heard his message loud and clear. Do not rock the boat.

"I will do my best not to disappoint you, Mr. Watson."

She walked away without letting him respond. She had to compose herself before she faced the children. She couldn't let them sense her fears, that would be unkind.

CHAPTER 29

The next morning came far too quickly for everyone. The children acted out, partly out of excitement, some out of fear. Even the babies sensed something as all four of them cried at once. It took every ounce of patience she had not to throw her hands into the air and scream at everyone to stop. Mr. Watson, on the other hand, looked and acted so calm you would think this happened every day.

"Please write to me if you need anything," she said to the older children, but where would they write to? Something stopped her from telling them to write to her care of Riverside Springs. What was she supposed to do to help them if they did write? She didn't know the answer, but she felt strongly each child should know someone cared.

"Write to me care of Lily's sanctuary. Lily will pass your letters onto me." She gave the older children the address.

"Do you think I will get picked, Miss Bridget? I tried to look my best, but my hair keeps standing up," Sally asked. The poor girl had a horrible limp, the result of an untreated broken leg. Bridget suspected her disability would put some people off, but she hoped to be proven wrong.

"You look lovely and, more important, Sally, your kind nature will shine through. Any parent looking for a child would be lucky to have you."

The young girl beamed although there was still a flicker of unease in her eyes.

"Will I get picked? Look how strong I am, I have muscles." The lump in Bridget's throat got bigger as Charlie tried to flex his arms. The poor child was skin and bone. She wanted to hug him close and never let go.

"Some mother will be lucky to get you, Charlie," she whispered as she put her hand briefly on his head.

"I promised your ma I would look out for ye Charlie, I told ye that."

Bridget smiled at Daniel, thinking he was possibly the last child they would pick, despite his good heart. His hair grew in tufts as if chunks of it had been pulled out over time. His pock marked face looked better than it had done when he first arrived at the sanctuary. The dirt was gone as were the worst of the bruises he had been covered in. He had lived on the streets of New York too long not to pick up certain traits. She prayed prospective parents would see past the tough guy act to the wonderful young man behind it. She would have been lost but for Daniel helping with the younger children, particularly Charlie.

Daniel hadn't told her his background, but

she had pieced some details together from Charlie. It seemed Charlie's mother had tried her best to help Daniel, a kid she didn't know. He was just another street boy. She had fed him when she had food available. When she fell ill, she had asked Daniel to look out for Charlie. Bridget couldn't help but grieve for the wonderful woman who'd died terrified of what would happen to her precious child on the streets.

Looking around her at the children, she wished all the people who had any involvement in the future of these precious human beings could spend some time getting to know them. They would see that rather than being an unwanted group of something only slightly better than animals, they were often the product of loving homes. Homes where mothers or fathers or, if they were really lucky, both parents had done their best to provide a decent upbringing. But through illness, death, poverty, or other harsh circumstances they had been unable to do that. Of course, some of the children had been abandoned, others didn't know their real parents. But they were all innocents. Even the older ones who had committed some minor crimes while living on the streets, such as stealing bread or milk, had done so out of hunger. If only she could afford to give each and every one a stable home. But that was the stuff of dreams. She was in the same boat, after all. She couldn't provide for her family and was giving herself to some stranger with the hope he would provide for Annie and Liam.

She hugged her siblings closer, promising them and herself nothing would separate them. She would die before she would leave them in some town never to be seen again. As she sat thinking, she couldn't help but compare herself to those mothers and fathers who had dropped their children off at the charity knowing they would head west on the orphan train. Those parents were the brave ones. To give your child a chance of a better future even if it meant you would never see or hear from them again, took a special type of courage.

She spoke to every child and reassured them as best she could. The older boys didn't want her to say anything, she knew they were afraid their composure would break. The reaction of the older girls depended on their background. Those that had up until recently enjoyed some semblance of family life cried. But the ones who pulled most at her heartstrings were those who stared through her. The girls who had some experience of living on the mercy of strangers. She didn't have to ask what type of heartache they had endured, it was evident from their faces. At best they had watched their loved ones die. At worst, well, that didn't bear thinking about.

CHAPTER 30

The train ground to a halt and, despite expecting it, Bridget couldn't believe this was it. She carried baby Martha alongside three of the older girls carrying the other babies. They went to the hotel where they washed up and changed. The ones not selected would stay at the hotel that evening before going back on the train the next morning.

Mr. Watson led the sorry little procession to the town church. Each child had a parcel containing their other set of clean clothes. Few had anything else. When they arrived at the church, she was surprised to find it was already full of people.

The children seemed to turn paler, if that was at all possible.

"Children, hold your heads high and let's show this town what New Yorkers are like," she said as they filed into the church. A stage had been set up at the top, she assumed so the people could see all the children.

"Liam, keep Annie beside you at all times. Do not go anywhere without me, you hear?"

"Yes, but where will you be?" Liam asked, his voice shaking with fear.

"I will be here in the church, but I might be distracted with one of the other children. Just do not leave this place."

"I won't," he promised.

Bridget patted her brother on the head. She couldn't cuddle him with baby Martha in her arms. Six years of age was no age to put responsibility on him for his sister, but it was the only choice she had.

Martha slept soundly. The sweet child was fine so long as she had her blanket in her hand. Bridget kissed the top of her head praying the little girl would get a loving family.

The babies were dealt with first, leaving the children standing in rows. Bridget couldn't help but think of the farmer's fair her parents had taken her to many years before back in Ireland. At the fair, bulls had been held in pens waiting to be sold off.

With effort, she held the tears back. She walked up to the town mayor who was in conversation with Mr. Watson. To her relief, the mayor was a kindly older gentleman who seemed very committed to finding good matches.

"Miss Collins, this is Mayor Huckster," Mr. Watson said.

"Nice to meet you, Miss Collins. And who may I ask is this sweet little thing?"

"Her name is Martha," Bridget said. "Her new family is supposed to be waiting here."

"Yes, the Westbury's. Lovely family. Four

sons and no sign of a daughter. Mrs. Westbury is desperate for a baby girl. There she is now."

Bridget turned to see a young woman rushing up the aisle closely followed by a man and four boys, despite the rule that no town children should be present in the hall.

"Is this my baby?" the woman asked, looking hopeful. "Oh my, isn't she so sweet. Jessica, sweetie, come to Mama."

"Her name is Martha, ma'am." Bridget didn't think before she spoke, earning a reprimanding look from Mr. Watson.

Mrs. Westbury glanced at Bridget. "I would like to call her Jessica after my mother, but I can keep Martha as her middle name. Would that be alright?"

"Yes, of course." Bridget couldn't keep the smile off her face. This woman was lovely and clearly adored by her husband and sons. Martha would find a good home.

"Mrs. Westbury, Martha's..." What could she say, perhaps "mom" would cause an issue.

Some people believed the child of an unmarried mother carried the sins of her conception. "Her friend gave her this little blanket, it helps to soothe her."

Mrs. Westbury took the blanket and put it back in Martha's hands. "Thank you, miss, for looking after my baby for me. Can we go now?"

"You need to see Mrs. White at the back of the hall, she will give you the details such as our contact in New York should you decide to return the child," Mr. Watson replied.

Return Martha? She wasn't some unwanted gift. Bridget opened her mouth but closed it again at the look of horror on Mrs. Westbury's face.

"Return her? She's my child. I wouldn't give any of my children away. What type of ma do you think I am?"

Bridget could have clapped. She watched Mr. Watson carefully, thinking she spotted admiration in his eyes. He really wasn't as cold and detached as he made himself out to be. She wondered why he hid his feelings so well.

"A wonderful one, Mrs. Westbury. I didn't mean to cause offense," he said, "but some people are not as loving as you are."

"I promise you, Mr. Watson, this child won't lack for love. We may not be the richest family in town when it comes to money or land, but we are blessed."

Bridget wanted to cheer the woman on, but she held herself back.

"Jessica Martha is a lucky girl," Mr. Watson spoke for Bridget as she seemed to have lost her voice.

"Thank you for bringing our daughter to us. I can't have any more children, doc told me not to, but I so wanted a little girl. Thank you so much. I will pray for you."

Bridget had to take out her hanky and blow her nose to cover her emotions. Why couldn't everyone be like Mrs. Westbury?

"The first placement is the worst," Mr.

Watson said in a low tone so only she would hear. "You are doing fine."

Surprised he had even acknowledged her, she murmured her thanks. But then he was gone. Her gaze trailed after him to where an argument had broken out on stage. She quickly followed to see if she could help.

CHAPTER 31

*J*acob had his arms wrapped around his younger sister Lizzie. "You're not taking her, you got mean eyes."

"Move away, lad, before I take off my belt and give you a hiding." Bridget looked on in horror as the well-dressed dandy raised a fist. She couldn't see his face but judging by the look on Jacob's face, there was no way the boy was giving in.

"I don't care what you do to me. You ain't

getting your dirty hands on my sister," Jacob replied, his voice shaking but with fear or anger, Bridget couldn't tell.

"Why you little guttersnipe—"

Mr. Watson put his hand on the man's arm and forced him to lower his fist.

"Excuse me," Mr. Watson said. "Jacob, what is the problem?"

"Mr. Watson, this man says he wants our Lizzie, but he got a funny look on his face. I said he can't have her," Jacob said, glaring at the man.

Bridget held her breath, silently begging Mr. Watson to listen to the child and not to tear him away from Lizzie. She was all he had left.

"Now Jacob, we spoke about this. It is not always feasible to find families to take siblings," Mr. Watson explained.

"But he doesn't have a wife and Lizzie needs a ma," Jacob said.

"See here, you listen to the man in charge. Now Lizzie, or whatever your name is, you are coming with me," the stranger made a grab for her.

"No, she isn't. Take your hands off that child," Mr. Watson almost roared. "Jacob, take Lizzie and go and stand over there with Liam and Annie."

As Jacob stood rooted to the floor, Bridget took his hand and Lizzie's and moved them off to the side in the direction of Liam. Then she turned back to hear how Mr. Watson dealt with the man.

"I want that girl."

"You, sir, will not have any child as long as I am in charge of this group," Mr. Watson said, in a tone that brooked no argument.

"I am as entitled to adopt a child as anyone else," the man retorted.

Bridget could see his cold, black eyes and thanked God Mr. Wilson was there to save Lizzie.

"Where is your wife?" Mr. Watson asked. "Only married couples can adopt and only with my final say so. Please remove yourself from the hall before I have to call the sheriff, and have you removed."

"You God-loving half-legged varmint, you think you're above the rest of us. I will get me the girl. Just you wait and see. I have money." The man moved forward, his hand moving to his waist. Thankfully, the sheriff had insisted everyone remove their guns before entering the Lord's house.

"I don't care how much money you have, mister. Now get out before this half-legged varmint, as you called me, takes his cane and knocks the head off your shoulders."

Bridget couldn't believe her ears. Mr. Watson hadn't shouted, but his tone suggested he would follow through on his threat if the man didn't move.

The mayor arrived just at that moment. "Johnny Felder, what are you doing here? You get yourself out of here right now or I will arrest you myself. I warned you guys over at the

Mucky Duck your presence here would not be tolerated."

Bridget nearly fainted. The Mucky Duck could only be the name of a saloon. Jacob had saved his sister, with Mr. Watson's help. She hurried back to where Jacob and Lizzie stood with Liam and Annie.

"Well done, Jacob, for protecting your sister. We will all be getting back on the train together," Bridget said.

"Yes ma'am," Jacob replied, but his hand gripped Lizzie's tightly and his eyes were still glued to Mr. Felder's retreating back.

"That man is leaving," Bridget hastened to reassure him. "Lizzie is safe now, thanks to you."

Only once they were safely at the back of the of the room with her sister and brother, did Bridget look over at Mr. Watson. But he had followed the sheriff down to the front of the church. She guessed he was ensuring the man left. What would happen if he came back with his friends?

* * *

SHE MURMURED a quick prayer before going over to a couple who were talking to Sally.

"Miss Collins, these people want to adopt me." Sally's enthusiasm competed with disbelief in her eyes.

"So they should, Sally. You are a wonderful little girl." Bridget turned to face the couple, glad to see their eyes full of kindness. "How can I help? Do you have any questions for me?"

"I was wondering how Sally hurt her leg?" asked the man.

Bridget's expression faltered. She looked at Sally's hopeful little face.

"Sally was hit by cart when crossing a road. I've no medical expertise but I believe her leg was broken and never splinted. Her parents couldn't afford a doctor," Bridget said.

Bridget didn't add that Sally's father preferred to drink all day long than work to pay for doctor's bills or food. The man started to nod, his head going up and down.

Bridget must have given him a funny look as he turned a little red before saying, "I am a doctor, I should have explained that. I believe I could fix her limp."

"Oh," Bridget replied, wondering if he wanted Sally as a daughter or a test subject. The lady by his side moved forward, her plain face lit up by a beautiful smile.

"What my husband is trying to say, but putting it badly, is we would love to adopt Sally and give her a home. If we can help her limp, we will do that. But most of all, we just felt drawn to her. We think we could be good parents if she would have us."

Bridget warmed to the couple immediately, particularly the wife. The expression on her face matched those of the children. She really wanted Sally to say yes.

"What do you think, Sally?" Bridget asked.

"I would like to say yes, if you are really

sure? I mean there are prettier girls than me that don't limp."

Bridget's heart nearly broke hearing the small child dismiss herself. She took a step, but the woman got there first.

"Nobody is better than you, Sally. Not in our eyes." The lady bent down and cuddled Sally close. "Will you be our daughter?"

Sally nodded, her arms around the woman's neck. The doctor held out his arms and put them around both his wife and Sally.

Bridget's eyes were overflowing as she directed the happy threesome to Mrs. White at the back of the hall. Sally gave her a hug. "Thank you, Miss Bridget, for finding me wonderful parents."

Bridget was too emotional to answer.

THE NEXT HOUR passed slowly with a few more children finding homes. Not everyone was brimming with affection like the couple who had adopted Sally, but as far as Bridget could see, the children were content with the matches. She took advantage of a lull to escape outside to the privy. There she allowed herself a little cry. Only once she had composed herself did she return to the event.

CHAPTER 32

*O*n entering the Church, it was immediately obvious an argument had broken out although the people involved were using hushed tones. Bridget hurried over to help.

"I only want two boys. I can't afford three." A farmer, if his clothes were anything to go by, appeared to be trying to explain himself to Daniel.

"But sir, if I promise to share my food with him, will you take Charlie please? I promised his ma I would look after him. I don't want to break my promise."

Bridget edged over to support the boys.

"I don't know, boy," the farmer said. "I mean it's admirable you want to keep your promise, but he doesn't look too strong to me. He's just skin and bone."

"That's because he didn't have enough to eat. With good food and fresh air, he will be as strong as me and Steven, I swear to you," Daniel pleaded, his eyes so wide they dominated his face.

Bridget wanted to cheer Daniel on, but she said nothing. Instead the man surprised her by saying, "Don't swear son, especially in the Lord's House."

"Sorry, sir. But please don't split us up. I will do his chores and mine," Daniel begged.

Bridget had heard enough.

"Daniel, nobody is forcing you to go with this man. We have several stops ahead of us and I am sure you will find another family."

To her surprise, Daniel shook his head

forcefully before saying, "Sorry, Miss Collins, I don't mean to be rude, but I don't want a family. I got a ma back in New York. She's sick in the hospital. But when I get older, I want to go back and look after her. So, I am happy to go with this man. He looks fair. I just don't want to leave Charlie behind."

Bridget looked into the man's face. He seemed to be struggling with his decision.

"Can I help in any way?" she asked.

"No ma'am. I guess I just can't afford it. I have a large enough place, but times have been hard, and it don't seem fair if I was to take on the boys and not treat them as they supposed to be treated. I need boys who can help me work the farm. I don't expect them to work harder than me and they will get their school-ing, but I don't have room for those that can't work."

Bridget could see the man was sincere in his struggle. It made her feel for him. Here was a good man seeking the best for the children and himself.

Dear Lord, please help us, she prayed under her breath.

"Joshua, maybe I can help?" A softly spoken, well-endowed woman in her mid-forties stepped forward.

"You, Mrs. Freeman? But how?" the man asked.

"Excuse me for interrupting, Miss Collins, but my name is Mary Freeman. I own the farm right next to Joshua's. He is an excellent neighbor and his wife, Annie, bedridden as she is, is a wonderful person. I couldn't help but overhear. I am a widow, my husband died years ago, and I don't intend to take another."

Bridget kept her face straight at that comment, but it was an effort.

"I was thinking, what about if I offered to give Charlie a home? I have farmhands to do the main farming work but could use a hand with my horses and barn work. Would that be of interest to you, Charlie?"

"Oh yes, ma'am. I love animals. My uncle, he had a horse back in New York. Used to pull his milk cart before he got killed. My uncle, not the horse. I used to help look after him," Charlie replied eagerly, obviously wanting to impress the lady.

"I'm not sure if it is allowed, Mrs. Freeman. I mean, well, the rules say you need to be married..." Mr. Watson replied, making Bridget want to hit him. Those rules applied to people like the man from the Mucky Duck, not to genuine people with plenty of love left to give.

The woman, smiling in response to Charlie's reply, turned to frown at Mr. Watson. "I was married."

"Yes, I know but—"

"What Mr. Watson is trying to say," Bridget interrupted, "is thank you, Mrs. Freeman. Your kindness is more than acceptable to the Outplacement Society." Bridget didn't look at Mr. Watson. She wasn't about to let two good homes go because of some silly rule some well-meaning individual back in New York made up.

"Would that work for you Daniel?" the man called Joshua asked.

"Yes, sir that would be mighty fine if you could see a way to let us visit one another from time to time. Like for an hour after work on a Sunday for example? Not that I don't trust you missus, but Charlie's ma asked me, and I hate to break a promise."

"You won't work on a Sunday, Daniel, and you will see Charlie at church and at school. If Joshua is happy to let you come over to my house for Sunday dinner we can do that too. That okay with you, Josh?" Mrs. Freeman asked, her eyes sparkling.

"Absolutely, especially if that kind invitation were to extend to me and my missus," Joshua replied, a big smile on his face. "I can carry my Annie over on the wagon if I make the bed comfortable enough."

Bridget knew they had made the right decision and these boys would be well taken care of. She heard Mrs. Freeman's reply as they walked away, "You know you don't need an invitation."

Bridget watched as the little group walked down to see Mrs. White. She had a feeling Daniel was getting a new father regardless of whether he wanted one or not.

"You made the right decision, Miss Collins." Startled at his voice, she whirled around.

"You think so?" she asked.

"Yes, I was wrong to even question it," Mr. Watson told her. "Thank you for stepping in as you did."

"I hope you didn't think me impertinent, Mr. Watson. I have just been party to two—no, three if you include Sally—very happy new families. I wanted a happy ending for the boys as well."

"Yes, sometimes throwing the rule book out the window works best," he said.

Pleased to see that not only was he agreeing with her, but he appeared to be mellowing, she said, "Yes, it does. I was—"

Bridget's words were cut off by a bloodcurdling scream she recognized as Annie's. Picking up her skirts, she moved toward the sound, realizing it wasn't coming from the stage. It seemed every person in town was in her way as she tried to negotiate her path. Her brother met her as she made her way to the back of the church.

CHAPTER 33

"*B*ridget come quick," Liam told her. "This lady says she is taking Annie and I can't stop her."

Bridget grabbed Liam's hand and moved quicker in the direction of Annie's continuous wail.

"Stop, please stop. Mrs. White do not sign anything. That child is not part of the group," Bridget cried out.

"She was part of the group and I saw her first," said the woman who was trying to take Annie. "You can't just pick her now."

"I'm her sister and she is not up for adoption. Release her this second, you're hurting her."

The woman kept a tight hold on Annie's arm, her vicious expression making Bridget all the more determined she wasn't taking her sister.

"Mrs. White tell this woman Annie isn't up for adoption," Bridget demanded.

Mrs. White gave Bridget a look of disdain. "Her name is on the list."

"What? That's not possible. It shouldn't be. I didn't give permission for her to be adopted."

"It says a Miss Collins did, Maura Collins," Mrs. White said.

Bridget fumed, imagining what she'd like to do to her older sister if she were in front of her. "I will not agree to her being adopted. This woman isn't suitable to raise any child." Bridget made a grab for Annie, but the woman held her tight.

"Now you take that back. You don't know

me, lady, and you can't say things like that," the woman said.

"I know you aren't suited to having a child. Look at what you've done to Annie. Your hold on her arm is too tight. You could break it."

"Nonsense. Spare the rod and spoil the child. And it's the rod you'll get as soon as I get you home if you don't stop that screaming you little—"

"You let her go right now," Bridget warned. "Or you'll be nursing a broken arm yourself you old—"

"Enough," Mr. Watson interrupted. "What on earth is going on here?"

"This girl just threatened me. I want her arrested," the woman demanded.

"I did not threaten you. I made you a promise. You continue to hurt my sister and I will hurt you. Now release her," Bridget said.

"Ma'am, please release the child," Mr. Watson said.

"She's mine."

"No, she isn't," Mr. Watson said. "She is

Miss Collins' sister. I would suggest you choose another child, but your behavior does not give me reason to believe you will treat that child properly. Please leave."

"I will not. Who do you think you are, coming into this town and ordering me around? I will have you know I am the mayor's sister."

How could this evil woman be related to the nice man they had met earlier? Bridget pulled both children closer.

"I don't care if you are the president's sister, ma'am. You are not fit to raise a child and you won't have one of these children. Now, please leave. We are done here, Mrs. White. The rest of the children, and Miss Collins, shall return to the train right now. I will follow as soon as I have a copy of your records."

Bridget tried to move but her feet seemed glued to the spot.

"Miss Collins, you need to leave now," he said, his voice firm, but his eyes boring into hers as if willing her to gather her strength.

"Bridget, come on we got to go," Liam said, pulling at her sleeve.

Liam dragged herself and Annie off. With one last look at Mr. Watson, Bridget gathered the remaining children and made her way to the train station where they waited. Mr. Watson obviously felt it wasn't prudent to spend the night in the hotel as planned.

CHAPTER 34

That night as the children slept on the uncomfortable seats, Bridget was too restless to even sit quietly. She walked through the car checking on each child, all the time her mind was working overboard. How could Maura sign the papers for Annie and Liam? She hadn't even mentioned it to Bridget, despite knowing she was going on the same train. If she was back in New York, she may well put her hands around her sister's—

"Miss Collins, is there something wrong? You seem rather agitated," Mr. Watson said as he walked over to her, concern etched all over his face. Scamp whined as he came to lick her hand, the dog obviously picking up on her feelings.

"I am fine, thank you," Bridget answered.

"We both know that's not the case," he said. "Why don't you come sit at the front of the car? I have some lukewarm coffee if you'd like some."

"Thank you."

She wasn't sure why she accepted the offer. He wasn't the first person she would think of confiding in, but he was the only other adult. She sat with him, nursing the cup in her hands.

"The first day is always difficult," he told her. "I would like to tell you the next time will be easier, but I do not like lies."

"Why do you do it?" Bridget surprised herself by asking.

"What do you mean?"

"You don't seem to enjoy the work and, well, if I am honest, you don't seem to be suited to working with children." She wanted to take the words back as soon as she saw the amusement in his eyes. He was laughing at her. Stunned, she didn't know what to say. She had expected him to go cold or get angry. But laugh?

"I may not be as warm or outgoing as you, Miss Collins. But believe me, I am committed to these children. I try my best to find them homes, each and every one."

"But that's not enough is it? They deserve more than food and shelter, they deserve love and happiness."

"Yes, they do. But I am a practical person. I do not believe in fairy tales. There are the occasional times when a match is made purely out of love. For example, with young Sally today. But most of the time, the people adopting these children are doing it for other reasons."

"Such as?" Bridget was afraid to ask, but she had to.

"Duty, more often than not. Some genuinely feel they should offer a home to get a child off the streets. Others want to impress their neighbors, their church, or their religious elders by showing their charity by providing a family for a brat."

His ugly word stunned her.

"I apologize. I shouldn't have put it in those terms."

"It's almost as if you are speaking from experience," she ventured but he didn't reply. Instead, he gave her another lecture.

"If you want to stay sane, Miss Collins, you will need to toughen up. Think of the life these children had back in New York. Almost anything we can offer them is better than returning them to a life of squalor and neglect."

She didn't agree, but she didn't want to argue either. She handed him back her cup and stood.

"I shall see you in the morning. Goodnight, Mr. Watson."

She walked back to her seat and sat beside Liam and Annie. Her brother had his arm around his younger sister, doing his best, even in sleep, to protect her. She closed her eyes, wondering how many of the other children had known love like this before it was cruelly taken away from them. She was determined not to become like Mr. Watson. She would retain her heart.

CHAPTER 35

Carl watched Miss Collins as she took her seat with her siblings. He knew he had upset her, but the truth hurt. She was setting both herself, and the children, up for failure if she insisted on happy-ever-after endings for everyone. Sally, and those who found a kind, loving home were lucky. But, in reality, most of the children would end up living in houses where they were considered strangers. Not quite servants, not quite family members. They would be the lucky ones. The unlucky ones, well, he would do his best to ensure none of these children would experience that lifestyle.

He settled himself against the bench, knowing sleep would prove elusive. Every time he closed his eyes, his mind focused on Miss Collins. Not only did he find her more attractive than any other women he'd met, he found her mentally stimulating too. She wasn't afraid to stand her ground. The way she had stood up for the children today showed she had backbone. He smirked at the thought of her threatening the woman who had tried to adopt Annie. He could only imagine she would follow through on her threat.

So why had her elder sister left her to travel with the children? Why had she signed them away? And why was Miss Collins becoming a mail order bride? Surely, with her looks and personality, she would have had more than one suitor back in New York. He wished he had asked Father Nelson more about his traveling companion, but he was too angry to enter into conversation with his old mentor. When he had offered his services to Father Nelson, the last job he'd wanted was to act as an agent for the Outplacement Society. Not because he didn't believe they did good work. He knew they tried their best. But it wasn't the right role for him. He couldn't give the children the love and care they needed, his heart having died some years previously. Scamp snuggled closer into his side as he absentmindedly stroked his ears.

CHAPTER 36

The children who hadn't been picked weren't too upset on the first day, in fact some, like Lizzie and Jacob, were really pleased. But after a few more stops and the ongoing rejections, the atmosphere in the car was dismal. Bridget tried every trick she could think of to raise their spirits, but nothing worked.

"Why won't God give me and Jacob a family, Miss Collins?" Lizzie asked her one evening.

"I don't know the answer to that question, Lizzie." Bridget swallowed hard at the look on the child's face. She didn't want to give her false hope. The chances of her and Jacob being adopted together were low. Alone, she would have been placed ten times over with her silver blonde hair and sparkling blue eyes. She looked like an angel. Jacob, on the other hand, looked anything but, with his scarred face. Would anyone care enough to see past the disfigurement or even question how he had come by it?

"I pray we will find someone in the next town, Lizzie," Bridget said.

"If we don't find parents, will we have to go back to New York?" Lizzie asked.

Bridget had promised to be honest with the children where possible.

"Yes, love, you will, but don't start thinking about that. We have quite a few towns left to go first. You and Jacob may find a family in one of them."

"Maybe you should talk to Jacob and tell

him we got to let two families take us," Lizzie surprised her by saying.

Bridget remained quiet, waiting to hear the girl's reasoning.

"If we have to go back, they will separate us anyway. They will send Jacob away and give me to the nuns. I don't want to leave my brother. If we were in the same town, maybe I would get to see him sometimes? I don't want to live with the nuns."

Bridget cuddled the child close, only then realizing that Jacob had been listening to the conversation. She watched as the boy turned and walked away, his shoulders slumped. Dear Lord, why couldn't someone see these children had suffered too much already? They needed love and lots of it.

CHAPTER 37

That evening, Mr. Watson walked to her end of the railway car. "Miss Collins, I wonder if I might speak to you," Mr. Watson said.

"Of course, just let me get Liam and Annie settled, and I will be right with you," Bridget said.

"The conductor brought me a hot coffee pot this time."

Bridget just smiled. Coffee would be nice, but her stomach was roiling wondering why he wanted to speak to her.

He waited until she had got herself situated with a cup in her hands.

"Tomorrow is our last town," he said. "If we do not place all the children, I will be returning to New York with those left over. Usually, we would also conduct an inspection of the placements made for other children, but I gather your plans are different."

"Yes, they are," she said. "I am traveling onto Riverside Springs with my siblings."

"To meet your fiancé."

Her cheeks heated as he kept staring at her. She should look away, but her eyes seemed trapped in his gaze.

"Miss Collins?"

"Yes, sorry. We will continue on the train until Green River and then take a stagecoach. My fiancé will meet us in Riverside Springs."

"He must be a man of means if he can afford to take on two children."

She looked away. She didn't want to lie but telling the truth would be too difficult

"He doesn't know does he?" Mr. Watson asked gently.

"How did you know that?" she asked.

"Something young Liam said. What are you going to do if he refuses to marry you?"

"He won't," she said, refusing to consider any other possibility. She refused to think about her worries about her ability to be a farmer's wife. Surely it couldn't be that difficult. Anyway, she would learn. She would do whatever she had to do in order to protect her family.

"Aside from your considerable charms, Miss Collins, what if he simply cannot afford it?"

He thought her attractive. Why would that give her such pleasure? Her heart beat even quicker.

"I have prayed about this and believe God will find a way," she answered.

"You place a lot on that belief."

Shocked, she stared at him open-mouthed.

Hadn't Father Nelson said he was once in the seminary?

"I thought you were to become a priest," she said.

"I was."

"So then, how could you say something like that?"

"Because I believe it to be true," Mr. Watson said. "Anyway, my beliefs are of no concern. I am more interested in your plan for Liam and Annie should you find yourself deserted."

"What do you mean?" She tried her best to hide her dismay he had picked up on her concerns. There was a very real chance Brian Curran wouldn't marry her, she had deceived him after all by bringing her siblings.

"If your fiancé refuses to marry you. Riverside Springs is, I believe, a very small town. What if you cannot find suitable employment?"

"I will. I am a good seamstress and a hard worker. I cannot return to New York and I won't be parted from any more of my family. If that happens, that evil man will have won, and I might as well have stayed in that factory." She shuddered, thinking of Stephen Oaks. Too late she realized she had said too much. She stared at the floor, mumbling an apology. "I'm sorry, I shouldn't have gotten carried away."

He bent toward her, she could feel his breath on her ear, and put his hand under her chin gently forcing her to look up at him.

"Please don't be sorry you said those things. You must be running from something horrible if you are prepared to marry a man you haven't met. I wish there was something I could do or say to help you."

Looking at his face, she saw the look of concern in his eyes fighting with something else. Was it admiration?

Her heart leaped, but she clamped down on those feelings. She had promised a man in Riverside Springs she was going to marry him. He may not want her when he sees she has two children with her, but she was not going to be the one to break the promise. Mr. Watson's hand was still on her face, stroking the side of her chin, sending chills running down her spine. She fought the impulse to move closer to him.

A child cried out, breaking the spell.

"I must go," she murmured, pulling herself mentally and physically away. Mr. Watson, no Carl, was an enigma for sure but one she desperately wanted to know better.

CHAPTER 38

The next morning, everyone was in poor spirits as they walked toward the town hall. Some would say the train had been a success. They had placed some twenty children out of the original total of thirty-eight. Bridget held onto Annie and Lizzie's hands, thinking anyone seeing the expression on Lizzie's face mirrored by that of her brother Jacob would see the painful truth.

These children had already seen enough pain for a whole lifetime before putting them through parade after parade only to face rejection over and over again.

She tried everything she could think of to make Lizzie smile, but nothing worked. Instead, one large tear rolled down the child's face quickly followed by another. Bridget stopped walking. She didn't care if they fell behind the others.

"Lizzie, sweetheart, don't give up hope."

"I don't have any left, Miss Collins," Lizzie said. "I know this is our last chance. If we get adopted here, Jacob will go to one family and me to another. Or worse, he will go back to New York with Mr. Watson. I might never see him again."

The child's heartrending sobs tore Bridget apart. Annie was also sobbing, caught up in emotions she didn't quite understand.

"I wish I could tell you that isn't going to happen, but I can't. I pray you and Jacob will find happiness together. But if you do get separated, I know your brother will do whatever it takes to find you again. He loves you," Bridget said.

"If he loves me so much, why isn't he here with me? He volunteered to take Liam and the younger boys with Mr. Watson. He should be here holding my hand, spending whatever time we have together," Lizzie said.

Bridget could guess why the older boy had gone with Mr. Watson. He was only a child too and was trying to protect both himself and Lizzie from the pain he knew was coming.

"Jacob loves you more than anything, Lizzie. Never forget that. He has protected you almost your whole life. It's difficult for him to accept he may lose you today. His heart is hurting too," Bridget said.

"It is?" Lizzie asked.

"Yes, darling, it is. Now can you dry your eyes and try to smile? Show Jacob you are a strong girl. He needs you as much as you need him. He has to believe you will be happy. And you will, Lizzie."

"How do you know?" the girl asked.

"I just do." Bridget crossed her fingers. She prayed she was doing the right thing.

"Bridget never lies, Lizzie. You can believe her."

Annie's innocence made Bridget wince, but she hid it from the children. Taking their hands again, she walked slowly to meet the rest of their sad little group.

She watched as Lizzie, smiling as if it were her birthday, and she was about to get a puppy, walked up to Jacob and threw her arms around him. The boy picked her up and held her close. Bridget had to turn away but before she did, she caught a look of pain so vivid on Mr. Watson's face, she felt like giving him a hug too. Then the mask fell back into place.

She looked at the ground quickly, so he wouldn't know she had seen his reaction.

"Children, gather round," he said. "You all know the drill by now. We will walk into the hall with our heads held high. You are all wonderful and the families in this town would be lucky to have each and every one of you."

"Thank you, Mr. Watson," the younger children chorused.

Bridget watched them as they walked. Most of the children remaining were six, seven and eight years old, too young to be picked for working in houses or on farms and too old to be considered by most for adoption.

"Miss Collins?" Mr. Watson said.

"Yes?"

"Are you joining us?" he asked.

His words were cold, but the expression in his eyes was anything but. She saw he was finding this as difficult as she was. For some reason, that gave her the strength to move forward. The children needed her to be strong and she wasn't about to let them down. She didn't look at the townsfolk as she walked to the front of the hall to take her place beside the children. Today they stood where they wanted, not in order of age. Lizzie was standing with Jacob, a little behind the other children.

CHAPTER 39

A couple of the younger children found new homes and Bridget helped the local lady with their details before checking Liam and Annie were still sitting near the top row. They had stopped standing with the other children since the incident at the first town.

As she walked toward the group, she noticed an older, well-dressed gentleman talking to Jacob. She moved quicker, eager to hear what the man wanted.

"I will give her everything she wants, don't worry about that. She will be well-treated and loved like our real child," the man said to Jacob.

"Her name is Elizabeth," the boy said, "but we call her Lizzie. Ma preferred Elizabeth but...our da he thought it was too good for the likes of us."

"I will call her Elizabeth, it's a beautiful name for a lovely child. Would that make you happy?" the man asked Lizzie who just nodded. She seemed to have lost her voice.

"Do you promise to make sure she goes to school and learns her letters? Ma said education was good for everyone. I didn't learn much, but Lizzie is real smart. She's good at math too."

Bridget swallowed the lump in her throat as Jacob listed his sister's attributes. How the child kept it up without breaking down was beyond her. She made to move forward but a hand on her elbow stopped her. She hadn't sensed Carl coming to stand beside her.

"I promise to give her the best schooling money can buy," the man said. "As I said, my wife is desperate for a little girl. Ever since our Constance was taken from us."

"I don't want to leave my brother. Can't you take him too?" Lizzie's pitiful wail broke Bridget's heart.

"Lizzie, stop it. We decided, remember?" Jacob said. "You need a good home where you will be loved. You behave now and go with this nice gentleman. He and his missus will be your ma and da. I bet he has a big house and a room full of toys just for you."

"I don't care about toys. I want to stay with you, Jacob," Lizzie said.

"You can't, you're just a girl. You can't go where I go. When I'm rid of you, I can live my own life."

Bridget wanted to scoop both children up and run away with them. The grip on her arm tightened and she sensed, rather than saw, Mr. Watson shake his head. He was warning her not to intervene.

"Elizabeth, would you like to meet my wife?" the man asked. "She's waiting at a café down the street. She couldn't bring herself to come in here this morning."

"If you are so rich why can't you take Jacob too?" Lizzie asked, obviously determined to fight until the last second.

Bridget leaned in, wanting to hear the answer for herself.

The man's face turned various shades of red as he seemed to struggle for the words.

"My wife wants a little girl. She doesn't want any more children than that."

"Then I don't want to come with you." Lizzie turned her back to the man, but Jacob pushed her into his arms.

"Take her, sir, please. She isn't usually stubborn, but she is just scared is all. Can you write me a letter and tell me how she is? Maybe just once a year?" Jacob's voice faltered on the last request, but he kept his eyes on the man.

Bridget saw the gentleman's composure drop but only for an instant.

"I can do that, young man," the man said.

"I have to say, Elizabeth is lucky to have you to protect her."

"Jacob, I don't want to go," Lizzie whined. "I won't leave you."

"You got to Lizzie. Think of Ma and little Ben. They're looking down at you now and smiling. All Ma ever wanted was for you to have a good home. Go Lizzie, I will be fine. I love you."

"I love you too, Jacob." Tears flowing down her face, Lizzie clung to her brother. Mr. Watson moved forward to help release Jacob. He nodded to the man, letting him know he should go and take Lizzie with him. Her screams echoed in Bridget's head, but her heart was fixed on the young man in front of her. Jacob seemed to wait until Lizzie was gone before he crumpled into a pile on the stage. His whimpers of pain were like those of a wounded animal.

CARL PULLED the young boy into his arms and held him as both their hearts broke. Jacob sobbed, his overly thin body shuddering as he did so. Carl held him as close as he could, all the time silently cursing the unfairness of what he had just witnessed. What type of God would stand by as children with nothing but each other were torn apart? He'd never felt so helpless. Well, not since…

He sensed her beside him, smelled the lavender she wore on her clothes. She pulled Jacob away from him and held the boy tight.

"I am so proud of you, Jacob," she whispered to him. "What you did for Lizzie was incredible. Your ma raised a wonderful young man."

Jacob's reddened, tear-streaked face looked up. "Do you think so? I thought she would be mad I let Lizzie go."

"No love, she would understand you did your best for your sister like you always have done. You protected her, and now you have ensured she has a comfortable home. You couldn't do more for someone you love."

As he watched, Carl saw understanding seep into Jacob. His pain wasn't going to disappear overnight, if ever, but somehow, Miss Collins had managed to say just the right thing to help this amazing young man deal with his loss.

"I agree with Miss Collins," Carl said. "Jacob, what you did today took more courage than I have seen in most men. You should be very proud of yourself."

The rest of the morning passed without any major incident. All of the remaining children found homes. Except for Jacob. A couple of farmers tried to speak to Jacob, but if the hard expression in his eyes combined with the scar on his face weren't enough to turn them off, his insistence on silence was.

CHAPTER 40

$\mathcal{B}$ridget's heart ached as she took Annie and Liam's hands in hers and led the way back toward the train. Mr. Watson and Jacob followed her.

She shared the lunch she had purchased with everyone, but only Liam and Annie ate anything. She could see they were affected too. Annie in particular tried to hug and cuddle Jacob a couple of times. He didn't shrug her off but made no attempt to cuddle her back like he would have on the train.

"Liam, why don't you and Annie have a

quick game of chase before we have to get back on the train?" Bridget asked, hoping to distract the youngsters. She was desperate to find out what Mr. Watson's plans were. Would he turn back for New York or would he make arrangements to check on all their placements? Would he ask her to come with him?

The conductor whistled, announcing it was time to board. Bridget called to Liam and Annie when her attention fixed on a carriage. The occupants must have been trying to catch the train as the carriage was moving quickly. She ran to bring Annie and Liam closer, not that they were in any real danger. The carriage drew up beside them and the occupant ordered it to stop.

To her surprise, the man who had adopted Lizzie stepped down first, closely followed by a woman. She assumed it was his wife from the way he held her waist as he guided her to the ground.

"I am so glad you haven't left. I would never have forgiven myself," the man said.

"Shush, Charles. You did what you thought was the right thing." The woman's smile was so loving, Bridget looked away from such an intimate moment.

"I am looking for Jacob," he said. "Is he here?"

Bridget turned back to find Mr. Watson standing alone. Where was Jacob?

"He just stepped aboard the train. Can I help?" Mr. Watson asked.

"Mr. Watson, I assume? My name is Alicia Hawkstone. My husband Charles came to see you this morning and organized the adoption of Elizabeth."

"Where is Lizzie?" Bridget interrupted.

"Oh, she's at the house with Mary, our cook," the woman said. "She's in good hands. Mary is giving her a bath. We came to ask Jacob if he would like to come and live with us as well. We know he is a little older and possibly wouldn't be interested in being adopted but..."

"Jacob?" Bridget asked.

The woman looked confused as she sent her husband a questioning look. "I'm sorry, did I get his name wrong? Only I thought…"

"No Mrs. Hawkstone, Jacob is his name but your husband, well he said…"

"I only wanted a daughter," the woman nodded, "and up until I met Elizabeth that was the truth. My darling Constance died some years back and since then I have been grieving. It was only recently that Charles suggested adoption. We have been…trying, but without success. But having met Elizabeth and hearing her talk about her wonderful brother, I can't in all good conscience separate those children. What sort of mother would that make me?"

Bridget didn't know whether to cry or shout for joy. She just stared at the couple, waiting for someone to pinch her awake. Was she dreaming?

"Bridget, should I go get Jacob?" Liam asked beside her.

"Yes, Liam. Thank you," Mr. Watson

replied as Bridget couldn't answer. She still couldn't believe what was happening.

"Mrs. Hawkstone, Mr. Hawkstone, you should be aware Jacob has suffered quite terribly at the hands of his father. He protected Lizzie, I mean Elizabeth, often at great personal cost."

"If you are talking about the physical scarring on his face, my husband told me about it and that is of no concern to us. We do not care what the children look like but what's inside of them that counts. Jacob proved to be a loyal and generous boy today. He impressed my husband and, believe me, that is not something that is easily done."

"Where's Lizzie? What's wrong? What have you done?" Jacob asked as he raced from the train.

Mr. Watson caught him before he flung himself with fists raised at Mr. Hawkstone.

"As you can see," Mr. Watson said. "He is still very protective."

"Jacob, Elizabeth is quite safe. She is enjoying a hot meal and a bath," the woman said. "My husband and I owe you a big apology."

Disbelief clouded Jacob's expression.

"We should never have thought to separate the two of you. Would you consider coming home with us too? I know you probably don't want another set of parents but perhaps you could see us as an aunt and uncle?"

"You want me?" the boy asked.

The combination of hope and disbelief in his voice brought more tears to Bridget's eyes. Bridget wished she had another hanky as the one in her pocket was already soaking. Mr. Watson came to her rescue by offering her his clean one.

"Yes, Jacob we do. When my husband told me what you said and did for Elizabeth, I knew at that moment I would be honored to have you for my son. But only if you would like to come with us. I don't want you thinking you're being forced to forget your mother. She raised two wonderful children. I'm only sad we will never meet. Perhaps she and my daughter Constance are together now and smiling down upon us?"

"Do you think so?" Jacob moved forward, his eyes still cagey.

"I hope so."

"You really want me as a son?" Jacob asked. "I can stay with Lizzie?"

"You can, but on two conditions," Mrs. Hawkstone said.

Jacob reared back as if struck. "What?"

"You must learn to call her Elizabeth. I think it's more fitting, don't you?"

Jacob's face lit up with a joy so powerful Bridget almost wanted to shield her eyes.

"I can do that ma'am." Then he seemed to remember there was another condition. "What else do I have to do?"

"Agree to go to school. Elizabeth mentioned you both had missed out on a lot of lessons."

"Aw, man, do I have to?" Jacob asked.

"Yes, son, you do. Education is the gateway to a whole new world." Mr. Hawkstone's firm tone told them all there was no arguing that point.

Jacob seemed to consider it and then nodded slowly. Bridget had to hide a smile at his reluctance to go to school. After what had been in store for him until these good people had turned up, he'd had a lucky escape.

"Do you think at some point you might call us mother and father?" Mr. Hawkstone asked.

"Maybe. It might take me a little time. You know, to get used to everything. I am kind of used to it being just me and Liz—Elizabeth."

Mr. Hawkstone held out his hand to Jacob.

"I would be honored if you would forgive me for what I did earlier. I would love for you to join our family, son."

Jacob shook his head, seemingly lost for words. Then Mrs. Hawkstone threw her arms around him and hugged him close. Bridget heard her whisper to Jacob that he was no longer alone.

Mr. Watson took Mr. Hawkstone aside to sign the paperwork. Then he fetched some parcels from the train, Jacob's belongings, she guessed, although there seemed to be too many bags.

Mrs. Hawkstone chatted with Liam and Annie while Jacob sought out Bridget for a private talk.

"Do you think my ma would mind if I called that lady, mother?" he asked.

"No, darling, she wouldn't," Bridget said. "Your ma would be so proud of you. You are a wonderful young man."

"Miss Collins, do you think I could write to you. I mean when I learn my letters?"

"I would love that," she said, smiling down at the boy. "Can you write to Lily at the sanctuary as I do not know my new address yet?"

"I will, Miss Collins. Thank you for everything. I hope you get your family too."

Bridget hugged the young man close, thinking how much they had both changed since she'd first dismissed him as a ruffian.

"I am so glad for you and *Elizabeth*," she said softly.

He grinned and whispered back, "She'll always be Lizzie to me, but don't say anything."

Then she watched as Jacob walked with a straight back and a look of pride tempered by disbelief to his new family. With a wave of goodbye, the carriage disappeared.

CHAPTER 41

Bridget stared long after the carriage disappeared. She would miss the children but hopefully they would get their happy ever after. She turned toward the train to find Carl standing beside her, the expression on his face grave.

"Now, Miss Collins, it is time for us to part ways."

"Oh, I thought you were traveling on to Green River," Bridget said.

"No, that was only in the event we had children left to place," Mr. Watson told her.

"Now, with Jacob gone, I am free to return to New York. I wish to check on the children on my way back, so the sooner I get moving the better."

He couldn't wait to get away from her. He was practically running out of the station.

"Oh, of course. Well, goodbye then. Thank you," she said, holding her hand out. She willed it to stop shaking but it didn't listen.

He took her hand in his. "It was a pleasure being with you on this trip, Miss Collins. You have a lovely way with children. They all fell in love with you."

She looked up at that remark. He seemed about to say something and then the old mask fell down again.

"Do you need anything?" he asked. "I have already removed my things from the train but have left you the rest of the food. It's not much, you may need to buy some more."

"No thank you. Myself and the children are fine. Liam, Annie say goodbye to Mr. Watson."

"Why are you leaving now? I thought you were coming with us?" Liam asked.

"My job here is done," Mr. Watson said. "You are the man of the party now. Look after your sisters."

"I will." Liam looked so proud to be called a man.

"But why are you going? I thought you liked Bridget. You look at her a lot," Annie said.

Bridget nearly died. Mr. Watson stammered, trying to reply.

"Annie Collins will you get on the train please," Bridget admonished her younger sister.

"Why are you angry with me? You said I should tell the truth. You look at him the same way."

"Annie, now. Liam, take your sister's hand. Goodbye, Mr. Watson." Bridget didn't risk looking at him, and instead, more or less pushed the children onto the train and into their car. Taking their seats on the benches, she glared at Annie who simply stared back at her. Liam moved closer to his sister as if to protect her.

"I thought she liked him," Annie said to Liam.

"She does, but she has to marry the other man," her brother said.

"But why can't she marry Mr. Watson? We would get to keep Scamp."

"Shush up, you've said enough," Liam chided his sister who stuck her thumb in her mouth. Bridget didn't notice, her gaze was stuck on the view from her window although she couldn't see a thing through her tears.

CARL WATSON WATCHED as the train disappeared, taking Bridget with it. He didn't know how he stopped himself from jumping back on and telling her how he felt about her. Annie had been right in her assessment of his feelings. Could she have been speaking true of her sister's feelings as well? It didn't matter, she was promised to someone else and Carl was not suitable husband material anyway.

He walked back the short distance to the hotel they had stayed in the previous night securing the room Bridget had slept in. Her lavender fragrance lingered in the room as if taunting him.

Lying on the bed, his thoughts strayed to his first trip on the orphan train. He'd been ten when his ma died leaving him responsible for his younger brother and sister, alone in New York. The nuns had been quick to send them off to good catholic families on the orphan train. Chrissie had been adopted at the first stop. He had tried to find her numerous times, but nobody seemed to have any record of a six-month-old baby. He and Tim stayed together all the way until they reached the second but last station. There they found a family. That was one name for them. A family where duty mattered above all else. Tim and himself were expected to work all hours in all weathers with little food. Their new parents told them it was their penance for their parent's sins.

Eventually they had decided to run away. Tim was ill and needed a doctor. He kept wheezing all the time and working around straw and animals seemed to make him worse. So, one day on their way into town, they had hitched a ride with a stranger on his wagon. Something spooked the horse and the wagon had overturned leaving him with a permanent limp. The stranger and Tim died outright.

Devastated over his brother's death, he'd prayed for hours and hours for answers. He was returned to the same family who punished him for running away and blamed him for Tim. He'd tried his best to live up to their expectations, but nothing was ever good enough. Finally, he'd agreed to become a priest because the constant daily starvation and other deprivations became too much.

He had Father Nelson to thank for rescuing him from the seminary. The man had quickly seen he wasn't there because of a vocation but because of fear.

Carl drew his legs up to his chest and, for the first time in what seemed like forever, cried. For Tim, his baby sister Chrissie, his lost childhood, his ma, the other children facing what he had faced, but most of all for the loss of Bridget. She needed a man who was rich enough to take on her two siblings as well as any family they might have together. He only had the pittance he earned as a part-time teacher. She was the one woman he had met who had seen through his cold-hearted exterior and wanted the man he could have been. And he had failed her too.

CHAPTER 42

*T*hree days later

ANNIE AND LIAM ran from one side of the train to the other, looking out the windows.

"Bridget look, the sky goes on forever. There are no houses. Where do the people live?" Annie asked.

"They live in houses, stupid. Where do you think they live?" Liam said.

"Liam called me stupid. Tell him not to, Bridget."

"Be quiet both of you, I can't hear myself think." Bridget stared out the window, her heart in her mouth. All this land with no people on it. It was so different from what they had left behind in New York. She prayed the life ahead of them was better than the one they'd left behind.

"When will we be there? I'm hungry and fed up of the train," Liam asked.

"Just a little bit longer," Bridget said. "Now why don't you sit down, and I will tell you a story."

She'd told them so many stories since they had first started out, she was running out of ideas.

"Why don't I tell them a story and you close your eyes and rest. You look worn out," another passenger offered.

Bridget looked over at the woman who had offered. "Thank you, ma'am, but I can't ask you to do that."

"Oh, I would love to. I love children, but God, well he didn't bless us that way. Please. I would like to. My name is Caroline Rees, and this is my husband, Philip."

Bridget looked into her kind face, her eyes shining brightly back at her.

"Liam, Annie, this lovely lady is going to tell you a story while I get some sleep. Be nice for Mrs. Rees."

Liam and Annie turned their full attention to the other lady. Bridget hoped they would behave.

"What sort of story?" Liam asked. "Can you tell us about cowboys and Indians?"

"I tell you what young man. Why don't you come over here and I'll tell you about cowboys and my wife can tell your sister about girl's stuff. Would that be satisfactory?"

"Oh yes, sir. Can you tell me about Indians too? I heard they are really scary and they want to kill us white folk."

Bridget was about to reprimand him, but the man got in first.

"Now who has been filling your head with that nonsense? The Indians don't want to kill us. They just want to keep their way of life and we, the whites as you called us, have been so doggone stupid we haven't listened. Often, we left them no choice but to defend what was theirs. Someday maybe we can all live in peace. The Indians can teach us a lot of things."

"Like what?" Liam's expression suggested there was nothing the Indians could teach him, but the man didn't take any heed.

"Like how to survive in the wilderness. They only kill what they need to eat. They do not believe in waste. They can show you how to find food even when you think there is none. Their women can weave bowls from reeds to carry water, they can build shelter and provide nourishment to their families. There are countless things we could learn."

"I wish they could show us how to get food on the train. I'm starving," Liam said, his eyes wider than usual.

"Liam," Bridget remonstrated but her brother just looked at her.

"What? I'm hungry." As if to illustrate his point, the child's stomach growled loudly.

"Mrs. Rees has a picnic basket packed with some delicious food. How about you all join us for lunch?"

"Sure, mister," Liam responded just before Bridget got a chance to speak.

"Thank you very much," Bridget said. "You're very kind but we will be fine. We will eat when we reach our destination."

"Aw Bridget, that's miles away and my stomach hurts now."

"Please Bridget, if you don't mind me using your Christian name. My husband is correct, we have plenty of food."

"Thank you very much Mrs. Rees," Bridget said, giving in to the couple's kindness. "Liam and Annie say thank you and don't be greedy."

"Thank you," Liam said. "Do you have cake?"

Bridget sighed. Liam was incorrigible but

at least Annie stayed quiet, her eyes taking in everything. Bridget closed her eyes even though she was tempted to stay awake in case some food came her way. But it wasn't fair trying to make the couple's food stretch to three more people.

"Do the Indians eat grass?" Liam asked as he munched away on a sandwich.

"No, child, but they do eat berries, nuts, fruit, and other produce of the land. They can fish too. Why old Red Charlie, he was the best fisherman you ever did come across."

"You mean you met a real Indian? Liam asked. "Weren't you scared?"

"Of Red Charlie?" Mr. Rees balked. "Not at all, child. He saved our lives a long time ago. If you're going to live in this State, you have to learn that everyone is equal in the eyes of God."

Bridget could feel herself falling asleep despite wanting to hear the rest of the man's story. She slept for ages, only opening her eyes when the whistle blew, announcing a station.

"Oh my, I'm so sorry. I didn't mean to sleep so long," she apologized, wiping her face as she did so.

"Your children were wonderful. They kept myself and my husband amused. You are so lucky to have them," Mrs. Rees said.

"She isn't our mam, she's our sister," Liam said. "Our mam died, and our brothers got—"

"That's enough," Bridget interrupted. "You don't need to tell your life story to everyone."

"I'm not. I didn't tell them you're going to marry a man you've never met."

Bridget didn't know where to look. She opted for the window as her cheeks flamed. She could have killed Liam in that second. But to her astonishment, the lady moved to the seat beside her and took her hand.

"Don't be embarrassed dear. We all have stories to tell. The child didn't mean it. Children are honest, they talk straight from the heart."

"I just…it sounds so awful, Mrs. Rees.

Going all this way to marry a stranger," Bridget admitted.

"You won't be the first, or the last to do that dear. I will pray your husband to be is a decent man. He must be to take on the children, no matter how lovely they are."

Bridget looked over the woman's shoulder, but it was too late. The woman gave her a shrewd look.

"He doesn't know about them, does he?"

She shook her head. "I didn't lie. I just didn't get a chance to write him back when I knew the children were coming too. I just couldn't leave them to the orphan train. I know many children move all over the place in those trains but not my sister and brother. They are so young, and I promised my mam I would keep them safe and together. I just…"

"Shush, dear," Mrs. Rees said. "Haven't you been through a horrible time. But what if this man cannot afford to take on two children as well as a new wife? What will you do then?

"I don't know. Father Nelson said the Reverend who visits Riverside Springs is a friend of his. I shall turn to him."

"Reverend Franklin," the woman nodded. "He is such a dear man. Rather elderly to be moving between parishes, but he won't listen to reason."

Bridget didn't respond. The lady seemed lost in her memories.

"Three children I have buried on the ranch. I refuse to leave them now, but I worry about the future. It can be so lonely at times."

"I'm sorry for your loss," Bridget murmured.

"Thank you. It was a long time ago, yet it feels like yesterday," Mrs. Rees said. "None of our boys reached one year of age. It was God's will."

Bridget saw the woman's gaze land on Annie who was drawing quietly on some newspaper.

"Maybe this is also God's will, meeting you and the children like this. We don't live far from Riverside Springs. We shall make a point of coming to church on the Sunday after we return. We have plans to stay with friends for the next month in Green River. Geoff has business to attend to, and I can catch up with my friends."

"It would be nice to see a friendly face," Bridget said.

"The next station is where we all get off. You will have to take the stagecoach on to Riverside Springs. Look after yourself and the children. I hope the man you have come to marry will be everything you wish for."

"Thank you," Bridget replied automatically. What did she wish for? Someone who would provide her and the children with a home. That wasn't asking for much was it?

CHAPTER 43

*B*rian paced back and forth on the street. The stagecoach was late. Not that it was unusual, but still, it wasn't helping with his nerves. What would she be like? He wasn't sure Riverside Springs would hold a lot of attraction for a city girl. And what about him? He had washed up and was wearing his best clothes, but he still looked and felt like a cowboy. Not some city slicker with fancy clothes and a full wallet. He didn't even have a family to offer her, not with him being an orphan.

He stopped his line of thinking, knowing he was just being silly. If she wanted all that, she wouldn't be coming to Wyoming as a mail order bride.

* * *

BRIDGET ANSWERED the children's questions automatically as her heart beat faster with every movement of the stagecoach. They were getting closer to meeting her soon-to-be husband. How would he look and act? What would he think of a bride who brought two children with her? Would he be kind? What age would he be?

"Riverside Springs coming up ahead," the driver called out.

Bridget rubbed her hands in her skirt and pushed her hair back from her face.

"Is my face clean?" she asked.

"Sure," Liam replied, not even looking in her direction.

"You look pretty," Annie said, snuggling

even closer. It was almost as if the child sensed something big was happening even if she didn't completely understand the specifics of it.

The stagecoach came to a stop. Bridget didn't want to look out the window. The door opened, and a man asked if she would like a hand down.

She looked up his arm and into his face. Her breath stilled. He was smiling, not only with his mouth but his eyes too. He wasn't old and toothless as she had feared.

"Good afternoon, Miss Collins? I'm Brian Curran."

"Nice to meet you, Mr. Curran," she said.

"Children, where are your parents? Surely you didn't travel on the stagecoach alone?" he asked Liam and Annie.

"No, they didn't," Bridget answered for them, finding her voice. "They came with me."

She couldn't drag her eyes from his face even as his eyes closed, and his mouth drew into a thin line. It was obvious he wasn't happy, but he wouldn't be cruel enough to send them away, would he?

CHAPTER 44

$\mathcal{H}$is bride had brought young children with her. What was he going to do? He didn't have the money to support a family. Not at the moment, and perhaps never. He looked away from the beseeching look in Bridget's eyes. How could he tell her they couldn't stay? Would she leave too? He had only just met her, but he knew he didn't want her to go.

"I'm very sorry, Mr. Curran. I didn't know what else to do. They were talking about sending them on the orphan train. You may not be familiar—"

"I know about orphan trains," he said.

"Then you can understand why I couldn't do it," she pleaded. "I promised my mam I would keep us together."

"Bridget, don't let the horrible man send us away. I want to stay with you," Liam begged her.

"Liam don't call people names. It's not nice."

"He's not being nice. Look at the way he's looking at us. We can't smell that bad. The Reeses on the train liked us."

"Who?" Brian asked.

"We met a couple on the train," Bridget explained. "Mr. and Mrs. Rees. They helped with Annie and Liam while I rested a little. They said they would come to church on Sunday."

"I don't think I know them," Brian said.

"They don't live far from here they said. They know Reverend Franklin." Bridget paused before adding, "I can look for a job.

The extra money could be used to support the children."

"You won't have time for a job," Brian said. "I don't mean to be harsh, Miss Collins, but the farm will take up all of your time. There are cows to be milked, sheep to be looked after, the household chores, baking and whatnot."

He couldn't look her in the eye as he knew what he was saying was probably breaking her heart.

"Please, Mr. Curran. I can't separate my family. The children, they're only four and six. How could you ask me to give them to strangers?"

"I'm not the one doing the asking. I didn't know anything about them until you turned up here. If you had written, maybe I could have made arrangements." Even as he said the words, Brian knew he wouldn't have been able to do anything of the sort. He had no way of providing for children and Riverside Springs wasn't a big enough town. There was barely a school and a church. The road called Main Street earned its name by being the only street in town. This wasn't New York.

WHAT SORT of life were they running from to leave New York and come to a place like this? To marry a stranger and risk taking two children all that way. Brian looked at her closely. She didn't look like a flibbertigibbet, but one who took her responsibilities seriously.

"Morning, Brian, is this your new bride?"

Brian looked up in surprise as Mitch wandered over.

"Shannon sent me into town to get her some supplies. I think she figures on making you a wedding cake." Mitch glared at Brian, making him realize he hadn't introduced them yet.

"Sorry, forgive my manners. Miss Collins, this is Mitch Williams, my closest friend. He helped me prepare my, I mean our, land and home."

"Nice to meet you, Miss Collins," Mitch said. "And who are these delightful children?"

"I'm Liam. I'm six. That's Annie, she's four. That man doesn't want us here."

Brian wanted the ground to swallow him up as the child pointed an accusing finger at him.

"He made Bridget cry. I don't like him." Liam stood at the side of the street with his arms folded across his chest. If looks could kill, he would be stone dead.

"Well, I didn't expect, what I mean is…" Brian floundered.

"Why don't we all go into the boarding house and have a seat?" Mitch suggested. "It looks like Miss Collins and her siblings could do with some refreshments. Come on."

"The town has a boarding house? But I was given to believe it was tiny," Bridget said.

"It is a rather small town, Miss Collins. But it's growing all the time. When I say boarding house, I doubt it's what you would be familiar with, having lived in New York.

But it is clean and, more importantly, provides some privacy rather than having discussions in the middle of the street. In fact, I insist on securing a room for you, so you and your siblings can change. I remember traveling from Boston to here years ago. I don't think the conditions have improved much since then."

"You are very kind Mr. Williams," Bridget said. "But I can't accept your charity."

"It's not charity, don't concern yourself about that. Brian will work it off." Mitch smiled at Brian, but Brian could see the questions in his friend's eyes as well as a hint of reproach.

"Thank you, Mr. Williams. My siblings and I would be glad for the chance to wash up."

"Can we eat too? I'm starving," Liam said.

"Could you eat a cow?" Mitch asked. "I could take you out to my field and provide you with a knife and fork."

Brian couldn't help smiling as the boy's eyes widened in response to Mitch's question.

"You don't really mean that do you?" Liam asked, his tone suggesting he wasn't sure.

"No son, I don't. You may not be in New York anymore, but we are still a civilized people out here. Most of us anyway."

Brian knew that jibe was aimed at him but what did Mitch expect him to do? He couldn't afford a whole family at once.

Sighing, he picked up Bridget's carpet bag and followed the little family across the street into the hotel.

CHAPTER 45

$\mathcal{B}$ridget was stunned by the friendly greeting from the couple whom she assumed owned the hotel.

"How lovely to see young people coming to our town," the man said. "You must be very tired. Of course, we have a room available. A grand double bed and we can put a bed on the floor for the young boy. My name's Grayson and this here fine lady be my wife, Emily. I'm warning you though, she's from New York too so no doubt will have your ears bent asking for information about the folks back home. You wouldn't think she's been gone about thirty years by now."

Bridget just smiled. She didn't have the energy to talk. If she did open her mouth, she was afraid the tears would escape down her face. Why had she ever thought it was a good idea bringing Liam and Annie with her? She couldn't blame Mr. Curran for balking at the fact she hadn't come alone. He was right. She had done the wrong thing. But then, she couldn't desert her family in their hour of greatest need. Kathleen wasn't old enough to look after the young ones and Maura wasn't yet of sound enough mind to keep them with her. The thought of the innocent little children being separated and sent to different folk, to disappear forever, was too much.

"Don't give up yet. There must be something we can do."

She looked up at the man who'd put his hand on her elbow. How she wished her husband to be shared the kind heart of Mr. Williams.

"You go ahead and get sorted and I'll order coffee for the three of us in the lounge. Do you think the children might sleep? They would be very safe. Mrs. Grayson wouldn't let anyone touch a hair on their head. That way we could talk openly."

Bridget nodded her head in agreement. She ushered the children upstairs and helped them wash and get changed. The room was very pretty. The double bed had a beautiful quilt laid over it, the pinks and blues in the quilt being picked up by the painted pictures on the walls. The pallet under the window also looked very comfortable.

"Is this what cowboys sleep in?" Liam asked.

"It is indeed, young man. Every night out on the range, the cowboys lay out their pallets." Mrs. Grayson winked at Bridget behind Liam's back. "Are you wanting to be a cowboy young Liam?"

"Yes, ma'am. I love animals and being outdoors."

Bridget had to turn her face away. So far, Liam's experience with animals were the wild alley cats and other animals that roamed the streets of New York. But she didn't say anything. She didn't want Liam to think she was mocking him.

"Can you look after your little sister while your big sister comes downstairs to chat with the men?" Mrs. Grayson asked. "I will be back in two minutes with some biscuits and soup for you. I'm sure you're hungry."

"We're starving aren't we, Annie? We will wait here for you ma'am. Bridget run along. We will be fine."

Run along indeed. What age did he think he was, trying to boss her around? But she didn't reproach him. She knew behind his big man routine, he was just as a scared as Annie was. She hugged her small sister and whispered that she wouldn't be long.

"You won't let them take us away, will you, Bridget?" Annie asked.

"No, darling. I won't let them do that to

you." Bridget crossed her fingers and prayed hard she wouldn't have to break her word.

She stood and smoothed down her dress, wishing her heart would slow down. It was beating way too fast.

"You look very pretty, Bridget," Annie said.

"Thank you, darling. Now get some sleep after you eat. Liam will stay with you and mind you, won't you, Liam?"

"Yes of course. I am a cowboy now, Annie. Nothing can happen to you."

Bridget closed the door softy behind her, Liam's words echoing in her ears. Pushing her shoulders back, she offered up a quick prayer before descending the stairs.

She looked around her for a couple of minutes before she spotted Mr. Williams and Mr. Curran seated at a table in the far corner of the room. Both stood as she approached and only sat when she was fully seated.

"I ordered some food as well as coffee for

you, Miss Collins. I figured you would be hungry," Mr. Williams told her.

"Thank you for your kindness." Bridget wasn't at all sure she could eat but it would be rude to say that. She could feel both men looking at her.

"I should apologize and try to explain my reasons for my actions. I didn't mean to trap you, Mr. Curran. Only, I felt there was no other way out. I had to leave New York in a hurry. My boss, he made certain advances toward me." Bridget picked at the cotton on her dress as her cheeks heated up. She hated remembering what happened, the smell of his breath against her cheek, the forceful way his hands had dug into her shoulders, but it was even worse telling two male strangers.

"I am sorry you went through such an ordeal, Miss Collins."

It was Mitch Williams who spoke, but Bridget's eyes were drawn to Brian Curran's face. He looked furious, but with whom she wasn't sure.

"It is worse than it sounds. During the struggle, I reached out and found a weapon on his desk. I didn't have any other choice. If I hadn't fought back...:" Bridget fell silent. The men didn't interrupt but waited for her to finish. "I used a letter opener to slash him across the face, injuring his ear, which gave me the opening to escape. I believe the wound was bad enough to scar, although I didn't wait around to check. I ran as fast as I could. Mr. Oaks is a powerful man and has lots of friends. I had to take my family from the only home they had known to the local church."

"Do you not have any family who could help you?" Mr Williams asked.

"No, Mama died three years ago. I have an older sister, but her fiancé was killed the week before in an explosion at work and she seems to have lost her way." Bridget was sure her sister had lost her mind, but she wasn't about to admit to having mental illness in her family. "I have a younger sister Kathleen, but she is only sixteen and far too young to take on the children. She was also sacked by Mr. Oaks."

"What an ordeal you have been through, Miss Collins," Mr. Williams commented, sending a dark look at Brian.

Bridget felt bad Brian was being blamed. She turned her attention to him saying, "I should have written to tell you about my brother and sister but there was so little time. Father Nelson told Lily, she runs the sanctuary in New York, that Mr. Oaks was bringing charges against me. I couldn't risk being sent to prison. The children were to leave on the orphan train, but I couldn't bear for them to go without me. Father Nelson gave me a job as a temporary placement office. I couldn't… that is I..." She didn't continue.

"Some children find happy homes," Brian murmured, but his tone suggested he was grasping for straws.

"They do, but most siblings are separated. Liam and Annie have been close since Annie was born. Liam has always protected her and looked out for her. He couldn't live without her. Annie is so innocent, I couldn't let her go to strangers. I just couldn't." The tears escaped down her cheeks.

Mrs. Grayson came upon them before Bridget could compose herself.

"My poor dear girl, what is the matter? What have you two done to her? Come here to me, child. Let's get you upstairs and put you to bed. Whatever the problem is, you can deal with it in the morning. Come on, love."

Bridget didn't have the strength to say no or to correct the woman over the fact she wasn't a child. It was nice for someone else to take control for a little while. She followed Mrs. Grayson without even saying goodbye to the men, let alone thanking them for the food.

"You didn't eat a bite either. You go to bed and I will bring you up a sandwich."

Bridget couldn't think about food; her stomach was roiling and the last thing she needed was to be ill. She had to get her wits about her. Not only her own future, but the children's future was also at stake.

"No thank you, Mrs. Grayson. I just want to sleep."

"I am not going to argue with you but tomorrow you must eat a good breakfast. You are far too skinny already and will waste away to nothing if you don't eat."

Bridget didn't reply. Her eyes had closed of their own will. Last she heard was the door closing softly and little Annie's snores as she cuddled into her side.

CHAPTER 46

$\mathcal{B}$rian Curran stared after Bridget as Mrs. Grayson lead her away. He couldn't believe the amount of trouble the poor girl had dealt with and had a feeling she had kept some of her troubles from them.

"What a mess," Mitch said.

"Yes, it is. I can't afford to take on two children. As it is, I'm not sure I have enough money to keep a wife." Why had he written off for a wife? In fairness the cattle rustlers had struck after he had written the letter, but still. He should have followed his gut instinct and waited until he was more secure financially. But then he would be an old man.

Mitch rocked his chair back and forth. "You of all people can't send those kids on the orphan train. You know what it was like for us."

Brian stared out the window. He knew he had been considered lucky. While not accepted as part of the Moore's family, he hadn't been ill-treated. Not like Mitch, who had told him the story of how he and his sisters had been split up. All five siblings had been separated. Mitch and his brother had gone to work for a farmer. He'd treated them harshly, kept them from going to school and worked them hard until Mitch's brother died from a fever and Mitch ran away. His elder sisters went to one family after another, eventually ending up working behind a saloon. Last they had heard, Mary, the oldest, had been found in a river. Susie had been murdered by a client. Mitch didn't know what happened to their three-year-old sister. Any records on Annie Williams had disappeared.

"I know you think I should keep them, but, how can I? I don't have the animals or the crops to support them. Children are expensive." Exactly how expensive, Brian didn't know but it didn't matter. He was barely making ends meet. Losing the couple of head of cattle to rustlers had hurt.

"Bridget looks fine and healthy," Mitch said. "I bet you she would work herself to the bone to provide them young 'uns with a good life."

"Yes, but what about when our own young 'uns come along?" Brian glanced at his friend who stared back at him. "Don't look at me like that. You know as well as I do how much I want kids of my own. It's all I ever wanted, a family."

"Seems to me you got yourself a ready-made family right there. God does things for his own reasons. Don't you think it's a message the girl who comes to marry you brings orphans with her? Where would you be today if someone had taken you in and provided you with a real home rather than just a roof over your head in return for labor?"

Brian looked everywhere but at his friend's face. He had spent hours daydreaming with Mitch as to how their lives would have been different if they stayed in New York. Both agreed they would probably have been dead by now. But if they had been adopted for real and given schooling and allowed an education would they both be struggling so much now?

Only God knew, and he wasn't about to tell them. It was pointless thinking about the past and what could have been. Brian had no control over that. But his actions would affect those little children. How could he be thinking of putting those children back on the train to end up goodness knows where?

"Do you ever think love could grow between you and Bridget if you send her family away?" Mitch asked. "You think long and hard about the choices you make Brian. The Lord provides in his own way. You know that just as well as I do."

Brian returned Mitch's gaze. His friend had a much closer relationship with God than Brian did. Mitch didn't hold God responsible for what had happened to his family. He had in the past but all that changed when he met, and married, Shannon. Shannon had been another orphan train baby, but she'd been adopted by a pastor and his wife. The pair had loved Shannon as if she were their own blood and brought her up in their faith. Shannon continued to study the bible and seek out those who wished to discuss it in detail. Mitch was a regular churchgoer whereas Brian only went when he had to. Such as their wedding or at Christmas. Or that day he had come into town to consider his options and Reverend Franklin asked him to write to Bridget. He buried his head in his hands. Was it God's will she come to Riverside Springs with two young 'uns?

CHAPTER 47

*B*ridget woke with a start the next morning, the comfortable bed feeling empty. There was no sign of Annie or Liam. Breathing heavily, she quickly dressed as she couldn't go downstairs in her nightshift. She opened the door, calling out to her siblings, but there was no answer. She got to the kitchen and pushed it open to stand and watch in amazement. Her siblings were sitting at the table, both working on some slates. Mrs. Grayson came back in from outside, her face breaking into a smile when she saw Bridget.

"How are you feeling this morning? I thought a lie in would do you good. These children, they were as good as gold. Not a peep out of either of them."

"Thank you for minding them," Bridget said.

"It was my pleasure. Now take a seat and I will dish up your breakfast. Liam tells me you are a firm fan of pancakes."

Bridget glanced at Liam who sent her an innocent smile back. Little rascal knew well that pancakes weren't Bridget's favorite food but his.

"Can I have some more please, Mrs. Grayson?" Liam asked. "Figuring out things makes a man very hungry."

"Ah, to be sure you can. You can have as many as you want. What about you Annie? Would you like some more?"

"No, I am stuffed," Annie said.

"Annie Collins. Just say no, thank you, please," Bridget reprimanded her sister.

"No, thank you, please, Mrs. Grayson."

Mrs. Grayson laughed. "She is a little angel, isn't she? How I wish I could keep her. Both of them."

Bridget didn't look up from her plate.

"Brian Curran is waiting outside for you, Bridget. I suggested you take a walk once you finish breakfast, so the children don't hear your conversation."

"Thank you, Mrs. Grayson, but I can't impose on you again."

"You can, and you will. Some day will come when I need help, and I will ask you to return the favor. Now off you go."

She all but pushed Bridget out the door. Bridget didn't have a chance to do anything other than grab her bonnet on her way out.

He was standing near the end of the little white fence Mrs. Grayson had used to enclose her small garden. He scuffed the ground with his boot, then looked up as she closed the door behind her.

"Morning, Miss Collins, I thought we

better continue our conversation. Could we take a walk around the town while we talk?"

She nodded, unable to find her voice. She had to calm her nerves.

They walked in silence for a while. Bridget willed him to say something, but he seemed to be waiting for her to start.

"Mr. Curran, I should apologize again for arriving with my brother and sister and not advising you beforehand. It was quite selfish of me."

"Was a surprise, is all," he replied.

Gratified he was being pleasant, she attempted to explain her actions. "I didn't get a chance to tell you I traveled with the orphan train most of the way from New York. I helped lots of orphans find new homes, some of them very happily. But I also witnessed some distressing scenes." Bridget fought to control her composure. Bursting into tears wasn't an option when taking a walk so she gritted her teeth. "I could not put my siblings through that experience."

"Can I ask why?"

She glanced at him wondering if he had been listening to her. Perhaps she hadn't been clear enough.

"It was horrible. Some people were there to provide loving homes for the children, but far too many just wanted cheap labor. You should have seen the way they examined the children. Eyeing up their arms and leg muscles. One man even asked a boy to open his mouth, so he could check his teeth. I didn't blame the child one bit for biting that man's finger. I would have found it hard to resist the temptation." Too late, Bridget realized what she had said. She looked to Mr. Curran's face and found he was trying, but failing, not to laugh. Eventually he lost. It was a nice sound.

"Forgive me. I tend to talk too much," she said, not sure whether to laugh or cry. Her prospective husband seemed like a nice man but when she looked at him, she could only see Carl Watson.

"Not at all. I would have done the same

thing. I had hoped times had changed but it sounds like they haven't. I know all about the orphan trains, Miss Collins."

"It's different from what you read in the papers." Even though she tried to temper her tone, it still sounded harsh.

"I know that. I rode the rails back twenty odd years ago. The selection or adoption process you mentioned was the same back then. I was luckier than most. The farmer who took me didn't hit or beat me. Not worse than his own kids. But Mitch, Mr. Williams, my friend you met last night, his story isn't as happy."

She lifted her hand to touch his arm in sympathy but withdrew it just as quickly. He might be her fiancé, but he was still a stranger.

"I am so sorry. I had no idea."

"You weren't to know," he said. "You have only just arrived here, but many in town traveled the same trains. Shannon was adopted by a lovely couple, she's married to Mitch. She couldn't wait to meet you. She gets lonely out here away from everyone."

Bridget wondered if Shannon would help her plead her case. Silence fell again as they walked. Not being comfortable with her own thoughts, she tried another line of conversation.

"It is very quiet out here compared to New York. How many people live in Riverside Springs?"

"About a couple of hundred, give or take. It depends on where you draw the line. The town is growing though. We have a church and a school now, though they're one and the same building. We use the school room for Sunday Service. Reverend Franklin is a busy man."

Her hopes fell, it sounded like there wouldn't be much chance of finding homes for her siblings if Mr. Curran decided they couldn't live with them.

"Miss Collins, would you like to sit a while? I feel we should discuss our…situation and it don't sit right to do that on the street."

"Where?" she asked.

"I thought we might sit in the Church," Mr. Curran said. "Reverend Franklin won't mind and it's plenty quiet this time of day."

She nodded, her mouth too dry to speak. She wished she'd worn gloves as her hands were clammy. She followed him up the few steps into the whitewashed church. It was empty as he had suggested. They both took a seat and then sat for a few minutes in silence. Bridget prayed harder than ever.

"Look, Miss Collins, I am a man of my word and I don't want you getting the wrong impression. But I just ain't able to provide for three extra mouths. Times are hard here. The banks won't lend any money and, well, I was managing just fine until I lost a few head of cattle a month or so ago."

Bridget looked at his face, only noticing now how tired and strained he looked. The dark circles under his eyes matched her own.

"You are a fine-looking woman and a kind-hearted lady. I would be honored to be your husband. But…"

"You cannot offer my siblings a home," she said, dropping her head.

He played with his hat for a few seconds before he looked back at her. This time she saw the tears lurking behind his eyes.

"I am right sorry ma'am. I wish things was different."

"Oh, please don't feel bad, Mr. Curran. I didn't mean to cause you distress. This is entirely my fault. You didn't do anything wrong. I was warned nobody would want to take on someone else's children."

"It's not that," he said fiercely. "I wish with every bone in my body I could provide a proper home for those little ones. If I had the means to do so, we wouldn't be having this conversation. I would never willingly send a child off to the train but I just…well the thing is, if things don't turn around, I could lose my farm."

Shame rose in Bridget, threatening to overwhelm her. By thinking just of herself and her family, she had put this poor man in a horrible situation.

"Please Mr. Collins, don't say things like that. I know you are a hard worker. People in town have only nice things to say about you." She left out the obvious, that she had only met a few. "I truly hope your situation turns around. You have good friends here who will surely help you."

"Thank you for saying that, but right now I am more worried about you and those little ones. Annie, she's such a cheerful little thing and Liam, you can just see he has a wonderful mind, him asking questions all the time."

"You are a very kind man, Mr. Collins."

"So, I guess I don't need to ask you. You don't want to marry me, do you? I understand. I know I'd want to do the same. I wouldn't let my siblings go."

"No, I don't," she said softly. "But to be honest, it's not just because of my siblings," she stuttered, but he deserved to know the truth. She had to be honest. "I…well I'm not sure I'm suited for being a farmer's wife. I don't know the first thing about sowing and planting and things like that. I can milk a cow and collect eggs, we did that back in Ireland when I was very young. But you need a wife who can work alongside you, to make your farm profitable. I will have to find a job in town to provide for my family."

"I wish you luck with your venture and will help if I can. We could be friends, Miss Collins. I would like that."

Bridget smiled, "I would like that too, Mr. Curran."

"You should speak to Reverend Franklin," he said after a moment. "He knows everyone."

"I will." She stood, fixing her skirt as she did so. "What would you like to tell the others? I mean your friends who expected a wedding."

"We could tell them the truth. I cannot afford to marry."

"No, let's not do that. I don't mean we should lie, but perhaps we could say we have decided we are not compatible." Bridget spoke quickly not thinking about the impact of her words.

"I think that might be a lie as well. At least on my part."

Bridget's cheeks heated up at the look he gave her, but it was gone as quickly as it arrived. On impulse she gave him a quick hug.

"Someday a woman will be lucky to have you as a husband," she told him.

"Maybe you could help me with that as well," he said.

Stunned, she waited for him to explain.

"If I can turn things around with the farm, maybe you can find a girl who knows how to plant and do farming stuff who needs a fresh chance. One willing to come out here to Riverside Springs."

"You know Mr. Curran, I might not be able to help with that, but I know a lady who can."

He smiled at her and she was filled with fondness for this gentle, kind man.

"So, do you think we could dispense with

the Mr. Curran and you could just call me Brian?"

"Yes, Brian. If you call me Bridget."

They walked out of the church both smiling. Bridget couldn't help but feel things had a way of turning out for the best. She would write to Lily and get her friend to start looking for the right girl for Brian. In the meantime, she had to find Reverend Franklin and see what he thought of the next part of her plan. Would he write to Father Nelson and convince him to let her try to stay in Riverside Springs?

* * *

TOGETHER THEY WENT to speak to the Reverend. She glanced at Brian as they walked to the house. His worried expression mirrored her feelings. He seemed just as nervous as she was. Would the Reverend turn out to be like priests she had known back in New York? Those that insisted on doing the right thing even if it was wrong for everyone involved. Brian couldn't afford to take on a family and she didn't want to live in Riverside Springs. Her heart and mind were engaged elsewhere.

Brian swallowed loudly doing nothing for her nerves as he knocked on the door of a small house set back from the street. The front garden was full of flowers, obviously someone was a keen gardener. The white picket fence surrounding the property combined with flower baskets on the windows suggested the Reverend was married. Maybe he would be more understanding of why couples shouldn't marry.

The door opened, and her heart nearly beat out of her chest. She rubbed her hands self-consciously in her dress not wanting to subject the Reverend to a wet, clammy handshake.

He was older than she had expected. The laughter lines on his face combined with the gentle look in his eyes helped to steady her nerves. He didn't look like the type of man who would order her to do something she didn't want to do. Did he?

"Come in, please. My wife is away for a

few days visiting with family. So I can't offer you home-baked cookies, but I can make a pot of coffee if you would like some."

'Thank you Reverend but we don't need anything but a moment of your time. We have something to tell you," Brian spoke.

Bridget followed the men into a drawing room littered with papers.

"If my darling wife was here, she would be quite annoyed at the mess. But I find it easier to write my sermons in here. It helps relax my mind," the Reverend apologized as he moved papers for Bridget to sit down.

The room was comfortably furnished although the furniture was old and well used. Mrs. Franklin or someone in her family liked to sew. The chairs had embroidered chair backs and the sampler above the fireplace was beautifully stitched.

"Miss Collins, Bridget if I may, it is lovely to meet you. Father Nelson told me all about you in his letters. You did a wonderful thing, helping the orphans find homes."

"Thank you, Reverend."

"Now what can I do for you fine folks?" he asked.

Bridget looked to Brian to find him staring at her. Perhaps she should explain.

"Reverend, as you know we, I mean I came here on the understanding I would marry Brian, I mean Mr. Curran," Bridget stuttered. "I, that is we, agreed it would be best not to proceed with our wedding."

The Reverend didn't speak but looked to Brian who nodded furiously. Bridget was tempted to reach out and stop him. Instead she clasped her hands on top of her skirt.

"Might I ask why?"

Bridget looked to Brian for help.

"Bridget, I mean Miss Collins brought her siblings with her. She was desperate to find them all a happy home. I...I just..." Brian's cheeks reddened.

"I put Mr. Curran into an impossible situation. It was wrong of me to assume he would be able to take on three new people. It is not his fault but mine."

"It's not your fault. You were doing what you felt right, Bridget. You couldn't let those kids go to strangers. I understand that,"

Bridget glanced at the Reverend who instead of looking angry, looked saddened.

"Miss Collins, I am sorry you found yourself in the position of being orphaned and having responsibility for younger siblings. It is to your credit you tried to do what was best for them. Brian, I admire you for your honesty. Given the cattle rustling and current economic conditions, I know it is not possible for you to take on a new family." The Reverend took a second as if to collect his thoughts. "It is obvious to me that you both have discussed this at length and come to a mutual amicable agreement and for that I congratulate you. It takes courage not to do something that is expected. Marriage is not to be entered into lightly."

"You agree with us?" Bridget clarified she had understood him but glancing at Brian's face she could see his relief.

"Yes Miss Collins, I believe you have made a wise decision. Brian is a wonderful young man and at some point, he will be able to provide for a family just not now. But tell me, what are your plans for the children? And for yourself?"

Brian stood up. "I should leave you to have this conversation in private."

"No please don't go, Brian," Bridget asked afraid to lose her ally despite the kindness of the Reverend. "I am not sure of my plans yet, Reverend. I would like to see if I can find employment and support my siblings myself. I have a small amount of savings to cover our expenses for a couple of weeks."

She saw the doubt in his eyes, but she kept talking to prevent him suggesting she send the children back on the orphan train.

"I know Father Nelson believes the best thing is for the children to be adopted and he may be right, but I want to prove to myself and to Liam and Annie that I tried my best to keep our family together."

"Your intentions are noble Miss Collins, but I am afraid our town might not be able to meet your needs. We don't have very many openings. But I will pray you find answers."

"Thank you Reverend."

"Now will you join me for coffee and tell me how Father Nelson is. I have his letters, but it would be nice to hear you speak about him. I miss his friendship."

"He misses you as well, Reverend." Relaxed now the truth was out in the open, Bridget told the men about Father Nelson, Lily, and the work of Carmel's mission.

CHAPTER 48

Two weeks passed, and Bridget was no further in her quest to find work. Everyone she asked either had no vacancies or was reluctant to employ a woman especially one with two children. She sensed some didn't believe her story, but they couldn't think Liam was her son. Could they?

Mrs. Grayson had offered them room and board in return for help with chores around the store and some sewing work. Mrs. Grayson had provided a repair service, but she complained she couldn't see well enough to sew anymore. Bridget thought she was making her eyesight sound worse than it was, but she wasn't too proud to accept a little bit of charity.

She didn't mind sewing by hand, her stitches may not be as neat as Kathleen's, but the time spent in the sanctuary had given her enough experience to do the job well. She was sitting in the store during a quiet period with her sewing. Mr. Grayson had gone out to deliver an order and she was alone with her thoughts. She had to face facts. There was simply no way she could keep her family together. She had to let Liam and Annie be adopted. It wasn't fair to anyone to let the current situation continue. She couldn't live off Mr and Mrs. Grayson forever. Nor did she want to. Every night she dreamed of children crying, begging her to help them. The dreams were so vivid she woke up crying out in her sleep. Brian had already commented she was getting black circles under her eyes, one of his less favorable comments over the last week.

"You have a neat hand, Bridget," Mrs.

Grayson said, stepping up behind her and examining her work.

"Thank you, Mrs. Grayson. Ma was a seamstress up at the big house when we lived back in Ireland. She showed us all how to stitch. My sister Kathleen she is a natural. You should see her work."

"Maybe I will someday."

She looked at her new friend and wondered if she could ask her to help Kathleen. Mrs. Grayson looked up and smiled, her kind eyes looking as if they might reach into Bridget's head and read her thoughts.

"You are leaving, aren't you?" the older woman asked her kindly, but her eyes showed concern.

"I have to. I can't find a way to keep the family together. Lily and Father Nelson were right. I had too much pride thinking I could do it."

"Don't talk like that about yourself, Bridget. You tried to keep your family together. That's a good thing. Few nineteen-year olds would even consider it. It's a pity the town isn't bigger. What will you do?"

Bridget outlined her plan to speak to the Reeses about adopting Liam and Annie. "I hope I didn't misunderstand their interest."

"From what I know of them you didn't. They will make lovely parents. You will find out soon enough when you ask them. But if the children are adopted what shall you do Bridget? You could stay here?"

Impulsively she put her sewing down and hugged the other woman. "I was lucky to meet you Mrs. Grayson but you are too kind. I, well, I think I would like to work as a placing agent to help the children."

"You want to help orphan children find homes?" Her incredulity made her voice squeak a little.

Flustered Bridget tried her best to explain. "I've been having dreams every night about the children. After seeing what I saw, I think I can help. I hope that doesn't sound prideful, but I know from experience how horrible it can be. I feel, quite strongly, the placing agents should have more authority than they do currently. I want to go back to New York and speak to Father Nelson. I want him to explain to the people in charge that these children need properly vetted homes. They're not stray animals to be placed with just anyone."

Mrs. Grayson stared at her in silence before she smiled such a warm smile, Bridget was tempted to close her eyes.

"I think that is a wonderful decision. You were born to help others, Bridget. It's your calling. In time I hope you find a man worthy of you if you wish for a home of your own. Those children, God help them, need people just like you."

"Thank you, Mrs. Grayson. I hope you are right. Liam and Annie may not understand."

"Not at first but they will in time. What of your other sisters?"

"I wanted to ask you about that. Mrs. Grayson, do you think there would be enough money from sewing to make a living just for one person? I know I can't support myself and the children, but I was thinking of my sister, Kathleen. She would be safe here. Away from the Oakses."

Bridget had found herself confiding in Mrs. Grayson. She'd told her the truth about her reasons to leave New York and her experiences on the orphan train.

"Is your sister as willing and able as you are?" Mrs. Grayson asked.

"Kathleen is much more able and has a much nicer personality, too. She is a real sweetheart but far too soft for New York."

"Do you think she would like to come and live here? I mean with me and Mr. Grayson. I like having someone to talk to. I am not talking about charity," Mrs Grayson hastened to add as if she was afraid of offending Bridget. "If your sister is as good as you say, then perhaps we could work together. I could sell her the material from the store at a good price and she could then make dresses and shirts for the people of the town. In time I think she could have a nice little business. But at the start, she could help me in the store and around the house if she wasn't busy sewing. What do you think?"

"Oh, Mrs. Grayson, if you're sure, Kathleen would love to come here. She was so brave staying with Lily at the sanctuary when we moved here. But I know she must be incredibly lonely for Annie and Liam. If she lived here, she could see the children at church."

"I am sure the Reeses would welcome her to their home for regular visits, given the circumstances. They are a fine Christian couple."

Bridget put down her sewing and moved to give the older woman a hug.

"I think I was blessed the day I came to this town. I already have so many new friends. I almost wish I was staying here too."

"You have a calling, Bridget. Maybe in time, after a few more trips, you can come here and settle down. Who knows, maybe Riverside Springs will prosper and be able to provide a home for some of your orphans? But, I think God wants you to work with the children for now."

"Do you? That's what I thought, but I didn't know if that was my pride talking."

"Sweet girl, I don't believe you have a prideful bone in your body."

THE WEEKS PASSED QUICKLY with the children settling in very well. She had started them at school, so they could make some friends. It also gave her some free time to write her letters to Father Nelson, Lily and also to Kathleen.

She told them about the people she had met. Riverside Springs might be a small town, but it was a good one. The people were friendly and had gone out of their way to make her, Annie and Liam feel welcome.

Mitch and Shannon had invited the three of them to tea in their house one afternoon. Shannon was a lovely woman and Bridget knew the two of them would have become close friends if she had been able to stay in Riverside. Brian had also joined them. He was like a new person now that he didn't feel forced to wed. Bridget understood Shannon was lonely, but she couldn't help but feel sorry for Brian when her new friend produced the mail order bride catalogue again.

"I don't need help from that," he told her. "Bridget is going to find me a farmer's wife."

"That's right, there are plenty of them on the streets of New York just lining up wanting to come to Riverside," Bridget joked, exchanging a glance of friendship with Brian. He had quickly become a dear friend, and she valued having him in her life.

By the time Sunday came, Bridget's stomach was so tied up in knots, she couldn't eat or sleep. She attacked the dishes in the sink to the point where Mrs. Grayson appeared to be concerned for her china.

"Fretting won't do you any good at all," Mrs. Grayson chided her.

"I know. Brian keeps telling me everything will be fine but what if they changed their mind? What if I was wrong about their feelings?"

"Goodness me, do you always ask so many questions?" Mrs. Grayson said. "You got to have trust Bridget. Haven't you learned that yet? Things happen in their own good time and we can't rush them. You will have more grey hairs than me if you keep this up."

Bridget scoured the pan, trying to take her impatience out on the scorch marks. Mrs. Grayson was right, but she couldn't help questioning what she was considering. Was it the right thing asking the Reeses to adopt her siblings? They would want for nothing if her impressions of the Reeses' financial situation were correct.

"Come on Bridget, dry your hands and get ready. Reverend Franklin may be easy going but he is likely to take a dim view of you turning up at service in a dirty apron."

* * *

BRIDGET MADE sure the children looked presentable, promising Liam a penny candy if he refrained from kicking every stone and twig on their way to church. She brushed Annie's blonde curls until they shone before tying her hair back with a pretty ribbon. Her siblings looked like little angels. They had no idea of her plans as she hadn't wanted to say anything until she knew for certain, she couldn't bear for them to be disappointed yet again.

They arrived just as services were starting. Taking a seat, she looked around the busy church but couldn't see the Reeses. Disappointed, she faced the front and sang the hymns. Reverend Franklin had a natural way of speaking and in the last few weeks, she had enjoyed listening to him, but today he could have been speaking in tongues. She didn't hear a word.

After service, everyone filed outside saying good morning to the reverend as they went.

"Good morning, Bridget and children, how are you this morning? Liam you get taller every day and you, young lady, look as pretty as a picture," the reverend said, smiling at Annie.

"Bridget bought me a ribbon."

"You have a very good sister."

Bridget wasn't too sure of that. She had been planning to ask strangers to take responsibility for her siblings. Who did that?

"Bridget, can you stop by my office please?" the reverend asked. "Mrs. Grayson will take the children home."

Surprised, she nodded before telling Liam and Annie to be good for the Graysons.

"You promised me candy," Liam whined

"I will give you two pieces, if Mrs. Grayson says you've been good. Now go on and look after your sister."

"Yes, Bridget," he said.

She watched as the two of them ran off, holding hands.

"Don't worry, dear," Mrs. Grayson said before following the children. "Remember every-thing happens for a reason."

She accepted Mrs. Grayson's advice with a forced smile before making her way to the of-fice. Opening the door, she found Mr. Rees waiting for her.

"Good morning, Miss Collins," he said. "My wife sends her regrets, she hasn't been feeling well."

"Oh no, I am sorry. I hope it is nothing seri-ous." Bridget felt horrible as her first thought was for the children's future if Mrs. Rees was ill, rather than for the lady herself.

"It will pass but she didn't feel up to dri-ving to church in the heat. Instead, she asked if you would come for dinner. Reverend Franklin will also be joining us."

"Oh, but I…" she started.

"Mrs. Grayson said to tell you to take as much time as you need," Reverend Franklin said. "Believe me, you are in for a treat. Mrs. Rees makes a splendid Sunday dinner. With

Mrs. Franklin being away, I am rather looking forward to a hot meal."

Bridget couldn't reply. It seemed as if everyone knew her plans but her.

She drove out to the ranch with Reverend Franklin, their buggy following that of Mr. Rees. Reverend Franklin used the time to ask her about the sanctuary.

"Father Nelson writes to me regularly. He is full of praise for Lily Doherty and what she has accomplished. She does wonderful work with the poor and the needy."

"She saved my life and quite possibly those of my sisters and brothers," Bridget said.

Reverend Franklin frowned at her story. "Bridget, have you given any thought to what may happen if this man finds out you are back in New York?"

Bridget had thought about it, but she wasn't prepared to let Stephen Oaks ruin her plans for the children.

"Yes, Reverend, but I believe I cannot let fear rule my life. Then he will have won, and he's already done enough damage. I may never see Michael and Shane again. Oaks may not be responsible for Maura's problems, but his actions didn't help. My lovely sister Kathleen was almost destroyed by his accusations. If it weren't for Father Nelson and Lily, that evil man would have a lot more to answer for."

"You are a brave woman, but don't take any chances. Do not underestimate this man or his reach."

Bridget didn't reply. She didn't want to think about Oaks.

"THAT'S the Rees place just ahead."

Bridget stared at the large house in the distance. It was larger than any other she had visited in Riverside and the surrounding area. The white-washed house stood surrounded by a maze of vividly-colored flower beds. The red barn stood some distance from the house, and she could see horses in the corral. There wasn't a thing out of place, everything was as neat as a pin. Mrs. Rees was waiting at the front door when they pulled up. A man, she assumed a farmhand, came forward to hold their horse as Reverend Franklin got down before helping Bridget do the same.

"Reverend Franklin, Miss Collins, how nice of you both to come. I'm sorry to miss your service this morning, Reverend."

"No apology needed, Carolyn. Something smells good."

Bridget agreed, the smells coming from the house made her mouth water despite her nerves.

"Miss Collins, it is so nice to meet you again," Mrs. Rees said. "Please let me show you around while my husband sees to a drink for Reverend Franklin."

Bridget had to keep her mouth forcibly closed as they took a tour of the house. Her eyes filled a little when she saw two of the four bedrooms were clearly designed for children. The beds were covered in quilts from which

Mrs. Rees had picked out the most prominent colors and used them to paint the bedroom walls.

"Your quilts are beautiful," Bridget said.

"Do you like them? This one is a family heirloom. My grandmother made it for my mother when she was a little girl and she gave it to me. I had hoped to give it my daughter…" The sadness in the other woman's expression made Bridget choke up even more. "I'm sorry. Some days are better than others. Today would have been our son's birthday. That's the real reason I wasn't at the service. I just couldn't face it."

"I am sorry for your loss, Mrs. Rees."

"Call me Carolyn, please. Now let me show you the rest of the house."

Carolyn showed Bridget the rest of the house, telling her stories of how she came to meet her husband and how they ended up living at the ranch.

"I love it here," Carolyn said with a sigh.

"The scenery is so beautiful and peaceful, but sometimes it's too quiet. I get lonely."

"I can't imagine living somewhere like this. I mean, I don't miss the smells and crowding of New York, but I like having a few people around me."

When they came back downstairs, the two men were waiting for them.

Geoff spoke first,"Darling, dinner will burn if we don't sit down."

"Oh yes, I'm sorry. I got carried away chatting. It is so nice to have another woman to talk to."

Bridget sat at the table, hoping she wouldn't let anything drop. The china was as delicate as that she remembered from the big house in Ireland.

"So, Bridget, have you and Carolyn spoken about your plans?" Mr. Rees asked.

Bridget nearly choked. She coughed and spluttered, causing Mr. Rees to pour her water while Carolyn slapped her on the back.

"My apologies," she stammered, her face

red both from embarrassment and the effort to breathe.

"Don't be, it was entirely my fault. My dear wife says I often open my mouth to change my feet."

"We love that about you, Geoff, so don't worry. Miss Collins, I mean Bridget, didn't have a chance to say anything as I monopolized the conversation. Why don't we finish our meal and then discuss the matter with coffee in the drawing room?" Carolyn suggested.

Bridget cast a grateful glance at her host. She tried, but couldn't eat anything more. Everything tasted like sawdust and made her cough more.

She was glad when they retired to the other room.

"Bridget, would you like to begin or shall I?" Reverend Franklin asked.

"No, please let me."

Bridget turned to where Mr. and Mrs. Rees sat on the sofa, noting they were holding hands. They looked nervous and, for some reason, knowing that helped her a little.

She opened her mouth ready to give her practiced speech when her mind went completely blank. The silence lingered as she struggled to remember but she couldn't. Panicking, she had to say something.

"I hope I am not being too forward. I got the impression on the train, you both became quite fond of my siblings. I wondered if there was any chance you might be willing to offer Liam and Annie a home." Her voice shook as much as her hands. "I have tried but failed to find a solution to our problem. I simply cannot afford to keep the children with me. To provide them with a stable secure life." Bridget stopped speaking as she tried her best to keep a tight lid on her emotions.

"Oh, Bridget, we hoped and prayed this was the reason you came to see us," Carolyn said. "We would love to offer Liam and Annie a home if you would be kind enough to allow us the honor."

"You would?" Bridget asked, wiping her hands on her skirt. Heart racing, she looked from one to the other. They were both smiling as was Reverend Franklin.

"You are right, we became very fond of them during the short train ride. We both wanted to say something to you, but you had your own plans and we knew you wanted to keep your family together." Carolyn furrowed her brows and then sent a sympathetic look Bridget's way. "But I gather it hasn't worked out as you'd wished, has it?"

Bridget shook her head.

"Are you going to get married? I take it your husband to be didn't want the children? Although I find it hard to understand why anyone couldn't fall in love with both of them instantly."

"No, it wasn't like that," Bridget explained. "Brian, the man I told you about, he loves the children but well…things have been difficult lately. He…we agreed it was best not to proceed with the wedding." Bridget fumbled over her words, desperate not to show Brian in a poor light but also not to betray his confidence.

"Brian Curran is an honorable young man who has fallen victim to some cattle rustlers," Reverend Franklin explained further. "They only got a few head of cattle but with things being as they are, it has put Brian in a precarious financial position. He couldn't afford to offer stability to Bridget and her siblings. I believe they have both made a wise choice."

Bridget gave Reverend Franklin a grateful look.

"Oh, the poor man. Those cattle rustlers have a lot to answer for," Geoff said. "We need a sheriff. I know Riverside is a small town, but we can't afford not to have someone in charge."

"Geoffrey. The children," Carolyn reminded him.

"Sorry, Miss Collins, I get caught up easily. I apologize for our remarks about Mr. Curran. It is easy to judge when you are not wearing another person's shoes. So, what, may I ask, are your plans now? Are you going to marry someone else?"

"Geoffrey!"

Bridget laughed as Carolyn gave her husband a loving tap on the arm, rolling her eyes at the same time.

"Forgive my husband, he is more used to dealing with men. He didn't mean it to sound like you would marry any given stranger," Carolyn said.

"No of course I didn't. Oh, I think I best keep quiet," Mr. Rees mumbled, clearly embarrassed.

Bridget rushed to reassure the kind man. "I don't blame you for thinking like that. After all, I did come across the country to marry a stranger. I learned a lot during my trip and in the process found a new calling. I want to work as a placing agent for the orphans on the orphan train. I believe the ideas behind the orphan train are good, but the actual workings fall a little short of the ideal." Bridget told the horrified couple of her experiences with Jacob and Lizzie as well as almost losing Annie. She also told them the happy endings achieved for many of the children.

"I believe we need to be more careful in vetting the families who come forward to take children. There are many challenges, but Mr. Watson, the man who accompanied me, is working very hard to overcome those. I would like to help him in any way I can."

Bridget colored as she sensed Carolyn Rees had seen inside her heart, but thankfully the other woman didn't say anything.

"We would love to take in your brother and sister. It would be a dream come true." Carolyn exchanged a loving glance with her husband.

Bridget could only imagine the pain these two lovely people had gone through losing their own children. She was certain they would give her siblings a wonderful home full of love.

"How do they feel about it?" Mr. Rees asked, his voice gruff.

"I haven't told them yet," Bridget admitted.

She'd put it off, telling herself she didn't want to get their hopes up, but the reality was she wasn't ready to say goodbye.

"Oh my, the poor dears," Carolyn said. "They will hate losing you. Not that we would like to lose you, Bridget. I speak for my husband and myself when we say we would like to adopt you as well. I mean you are too old to become our child, but we would love you to feel as if this is your home too."

Bridget couldn't believe her ears. "You would?"

"Yes, we would. We have plenty of space so if you decided to travel, you could come and stay with us whenever you wished." Carolyn moved to sit beside Bridget and took her hand. "You are giving us the greatest, most valuable gift anyone can give another: a family. We consider you to be a part of that family."

Bridget couldn't hold back the tears and soon both herself and Carolyn were sobbing.

"Perhaps you could show me that horse

again, Geoff. I rather fancy a walk," Reverend Franklin suggested, his voice shaking slightly.

Bridget and Carolyn exchanged a smile as the men almost ran out of the house.

"Men, they can never cope when the tears start falling," Carolyn commented with a fond look at her husband's retreating back.

Bridget blew her nose. She didn't know what to say.

"Forgive me for being nosy, but am I right in thinking Mr. Watson may have stolen a bit of your heart?" Carolyn asked.

"Is it that obvious? I wouldn't want Reverend Franklin thinking I'm casual with my affections," Bridget said.

"No dear, only to another woman. The men have no idea."

Bridget took a deep breath, glad to have another person to discuss her thoughts with.

"Yes, he has. I tried my best to fight it as I'd promised to marry Brian. I didn't do anything, you know, to show him I liked him. But yes, I admit to finding him intriguing and attractive."

"And does he feel the same?" Carolyn asked.

"He's an honorable man and as far as he was concerned I was spoken for."

"But?" Carolyn asked.

"Yes, I hope so," Bridget admitted. "I think so. Oh, I don't know. I don't have much experience with men."

"Will you write to him to tell him you are no longer spoken for?"

"No, not at the moment," Bridget said. "Other things take priority, such as getting the children settled. I have to go back to New York and check on my sisters. Kathleen is young and vulnerable. Mrs. Grayson has offered a suggestion and I want to discuss it with Kathleen, in person."

Bridget told Carolyn of Mrs. Grayson's plans.

"Mrs. Grayson is a wise woman," Carolyn said, nodding. "Not only will Kathleen benefit but so will she. The women in town will want pretty dresses, and the store under the boarding house is the place to buy material. Kathleen can come out to see the children. We would be delighted to have her, and I am sure the children would be thrilled."

"I think it will work out well for both of them. Kathleen would enjoy coming to see you and the children."

"Both of you will always be welcome, Bridget. If Kathleen was happy, would you feel free to live your life?" Carolyn looked her straight in the eye. Bridget couldn't look away.

"I can't chase after him, but Mr. Watson works for the Outplacement Society. So, if I follow my dreams, our paths are likely to cross again."

"What of your older sister? Will she be against this adoption?"

Bridget could feel her heart harden at the mention of Maura's name. She had betrayed her trust when she signed the letter allowing Annie and Liam to be adopted by just anyone.

"No, she won't stop it. Maura is glad to be rid of us."

"You can't mean that, Bridget. I know I don't know her but you, Annie, and Liam have been raised well. Your sister shares your blood and your parents. She must have a good heart too. Maybe she was frightened?"

Was it fear that had made Maura act as she had? Bridget didn't know but she didn't have the energy to wonder about that now.

"So, when will we tell Liam and Annie the news? Would you and Geoff like to come into town with me now to fetch them?"

"We would, but perhaps you would like to have one more night with just the three of you. I can send Geoffrey in to collect you all to-morrow and you can come and stay with us as the children settle in. If you aren't in a rush back to New York."

"I can stay a few days," Bridget confirmed. She didn't want to put off the goodbye for too long as it would only be harder.

CHAPTER 49

*B*ridget returned to the Graysons to find her siblings had been thoroughly spoiled. Mrs. Grayson had put them to bed with a goodnight story and they were fast asleep by the time she got home. She would have to wait until the morning to tell them her news. The night dragged by as she watched her younger siblings sleep. Would they ever understand how hard this decision had been for her? Was she making the right decision? She knew in her head she was, but her heart was challenging her. Was she doing this for them or for her? If she didn't have the children, she was free to work as an outplacement agent, free to go looking for Carl. What if he didn't want her? That was a risk she must take. She tossed and turned all night but sleep never came.

"LIAM, Annie, come here into the bed. I have something to tell you," Bridget said.

"Ah Bridget, I wanted to go downstairs," Liam said. "Brian said he would take me hunting."

"Not today, darling. Brian has to work. He said he would take you on Saturday."

"When's Saturday, is it tomorrow?" Annie asked. "I don't want to go."

"Girls don't go hunting silly. You stay here and do dishes and stuff," Liam said.

"Children, please don't fight. This is important," Bridget said.

She waited until Liam climbed into the bed, Annie moving closer to her.

"You know how we found families for the

other children on the train. Lizzie and Jacob had a new family and so did Sally."

They didn't answer but their eyes widened. Liam reached for Annie's hand, ever protective.

"I am not going to marry Brian," Bridget said.

"Why? I like him," Liam said.

"I know you do, and he likes you. A lot. You can still spend time together." Bridget took a deep breath, praying she would find the right words. "Do you remember Mr. and Mrs. Rees from the train?"

"The lady who told us stories?" Annie asked.

"The man who was going to let me meet a real Indian?" Liam asked.

"Yes. Geoff and Carolyn Rees live just a little way outside Riverside Springs. They have a beautiful home, with lots of rooms. They have a barn too and horses and—"

"Do they have cats?"

"Yes, Annie, they do. And dogs and chickens."

"Why are you telling us about them?" Liam asked, looking suspicious.

"Liam, they fell in love with you both on the train and they would like you to come and live with them. Both of you," Bridget said.

"You're sending us away?" Liam glared at her, disbelief and anger on his face.

"I don't want to go away," Annie sobbed.

"No, I'm not sending you away. They want to adopt me too," Bridget said.

"They do? But you're old. You don't need a ma and pa." Annie's statement would have been funny if the circumstances were different. Bridget was struggling to see her siblings through her tears. She wanted to gather them to her and never let go. But she couldn't offer them a life.

"Geoff is coming into town this morning and he's going to take the three of us back to his house. I can't wait for you to see your new bedrooms. You have one each."

"I'm not going," Liam said. "I want to stay with you."

"Liam, you have to come. I'm going too," she said.

"Are you going to stay there with us?" he asked.

Tempted to lie, Bridget knew it would only backfire on her later.

"No darling, not all the time. But I will visit as often as I can. I will write to you too."

"Where are you going?" Liam's accusing tone made Annie move closer to her. She held her sister tighter but looked at Liam when she spoke.

"Liam, I have tried everything I can think of to keep us together. But I can't find work and without a job, I don't have the money to provide us with a house or food."

"I can work."

"No darling, you can't. You have to go to school and get an education. I know Mam would want you to do that." Bridget took a deep breath. "Jobs are scarce in this small town. You will have a better life with the Reeses and they have promised I can come and see you."

Liam's expression didn't change. She kept talking, trying to make him understand.

"I am going back to New York but not to stay. I want to help other children find families. Sad children who don't have anyone else."

Annie and Liam didn't say a word but just stared at her for a few long seconds. Then Liam bolted.

"Liam come back," she called after him.

"No, you don't want us. I hate you."

Bridget couldn't move fast enough to stop him as the door banged after him. Annie sobbed as her little body shuddered. Bridget tried to cuddle her, but Annie held herself rigid.

CHAPTER 50

$\mathcal{B}$rian walked up the street toward the store. He had lots of things to do but he knew Bridget was telling the children about their new living arrangements today and sensed she may need some support.

He was glad he had as he spotted Liam bolt from the Grayson's store. He ran after the boy, afraid the child would get lost in unfamiliar surroundings.

"Hey, Liam, wait. I can't run as fast as you."

Liam stopped running away and instead ran

toward him. Next thing he knew, the child was aiming kicks and punches at Brian.

"I hate you. If you married Bridget, she wouldn't be giving us away."

Brian put his arms around the small, frightened boy and gathered him close, holding him until the fight left his body and the sobs came.

"I know you're angry with me but believe me I wanted you. And Annie. But I don't have the money to support a family. Bridget has done her best. She loves you more than anything."

"Why can't you keep us? I'll work hard as anything. I don't eat much either."

"Liam, look at me." Brian bent down to the boy's level. "I was the same as you once. My folks died, and I left New York on a train like the one you took. But I didn't have a big sister looking after me."

"Did you get a good family?" Liam asked.

"I got a home but no, not a family. Bridget doesn't want that to happen to you and Annie.

You met Geoff and Carolyn Rees. You told me about them, remember?"

Liam didn't say anything.

"You said they were really nice to you on the train and Mr. Rees had an Indian friend. Do you remember his name?"

"Red Charlie."

"Wouldn't you like to meet Mr. Rees and his wife again? Bridget says they're lovely people and she wouldn't let you go to anyone who wasn't nice."

"I don't want anyone. I want to stay with Bridget."

"She wants that too Liam, but sometimes life doesn't give us what we want," Brian said. "If you stay in Riverside Springs, Bridget can help children who have nobody else. She will come to visit you and Annie as much as she can. She won't ever forget you."

"Why did God let our ma die? She wouldn't have given us away."

"Nobody is giving you away, Liam. I can't answer your question about God, perhaps you could ask Reverend Franklin. But for now, do you think you could come and get breakfast with me? I'm starving."

Liam nodded. Then asked, "Are you still going to take me hunting?"

"I think your new pa would like to do that, but I can come with you if he says it's okay."

"So, you'll still be my friend?"

"Yes, Liam, I will always be your friend. You and Annie, you're special."

Liam scuffed the ground. "I guess I could eat some pancakes."

"Pancakes sound good to me. Let's go see if Mrs. Grayson has some."

Brian stood and together they walked toward the store. Bridget came running when she saw them.

"Oh, Liam, darling, I was so worried."

"We were just having a talk. He wants some pancakes." Brian motioned to Bridget to just leave it be. There was little point in admonishing the child for running away. His little life had turned upside down so many times, he was just overwhelmed.

"Thank you, Brian," she said.

"Don't thank me. I need pancakes too." He smiled at her. She was a lovely woman and would make someone a fine wife. But to him, she was like a sister now. Funny that. Someday he would like to marry but first he wanted to secure a future for the family he hoped to have.

CHAPTER 51

*G*eoff Rees arrived just as Liam and Brian were finishing their pancakes. The poor man looked more nervous than the children.

"Come in, Mr. Rees. Would you like some coffee?" Mrs. Grayson asked, her face full of sympathy.

"No thank you, ma'am."

Bridget guessed Carolyn was waiting for them on tenterhooks. She washed the children's hands and faces before telling them to say goodbye to Brian and Mrs. Grayson.

"Mr. Rees, can Brian come with us? To see your place? He's my friend."

"He can but he may have work to do, Liam."

"Do ya?" Liam asked Brian.

Bridget knew the mountain of chores Brian had. She was about to decline on his behalf but didn't get a chance.

"If Mr. Rees wouldn't mind, I would like that, Liam."

"I don't mind at all. And the name's Geoff."

"Thank you, Geoff. Liam and I had a talk today about going hunting. We'd plans to go this Saturday."

"Mind if I tag along?" Geoff asked. "I can't remember the last time I went hunting."

Bridget had to squeeze the tears back. Geoff was asking permission, yet he was about to become Liam's pa. She saw her younger brother soaking it all in and, for the first time this morning, a smile appeared on his face.

"Liam and Annie, I have something small

for both of you." Mrs. Grayson handed Annie a cloth doll and gave Liam a small bow and arrow.

"It's not a toy, Liam," she said. "Your pa will show you how to use it."

"Thank you, Mrs. Grayson," Liam said.

"I will see you next Sunday at Church."

The children nodded. Bridget gave her friend a hug. "I will see you in a few days," she whispered, noting the tears on the older woman's cheeks.

"Come on everyone, let's go," Geoff said, taking control.

Geoff secured their little case in the buggy and then they all climbed into it save for Brian who rode his horse. The little party took off with the children waving to Mrs. Grayson.

OVERWHELMED, Bridget stayed quiet the whole trip. Geoff filled the silence by pointing out to the young 'uns different things in town first and then in the countryside.

"Is Red Charlie at your house?" Liam asked.

"No, he's away with his own people. But he comes to visit sometimes."

"When?"

"I don't know when he will arrive. He just shows up, stays for a few days and then disappears again," Geoff said.

"Will he teach me how to use this?" Liam asked, raising the bow from his lap.

"I can teach you that, son."

"You know how to use a bow and arrow? Wow," Liam said, sounding excited. "Will you show me how to shoot a gun, too?"

"In time."

Bridget gasped.

"It's important all boys know how to protect their families," Geoff explained. "But we'll be careful, don't you worry."

Bridget would worry, but she knew Geoff was right. There were lots of wild animals around and maybe one day Liam would have to shoot one. She hoped that was sometime far in the future.

"This here is our land," Geoff said as they approached the large property. "You'll see the house shortly."

"You own all this?" Liam looked around him.

"Yes, son we do."

"Are they yours as well?" Liam pointed out the horses in the field.

"Yes. One of them will be yours and we'll have to get a small pony for Annie."

"You're giving me a horse?" Liam gaped at the man.

"How else do you think you'll get into town? It's a man's work, owning a horse. You got to treat it right. Isn't that true, Brian?"

"Sure is. You got to make sure you rub her down and give her water and oats to eat. You can't look after yourself till your horse is cared for. I don't know if you are old enough yet, Liam."

"I am. I am nearly seven. That's a man's age."

Bridget spotted Carolyn waiting at the door, the poor woman was rubbing her hands up and down on her dress and looking nervous.

Geoff pulled up outside the house allowing Carolyn to come forward.

"Carolyn, this is Brian Curran, a particular friend of Liam's. Liam asked him to come along."

"Nice to meet you, Mrs. Rees," Brian said.

"Likewise, Mr. Curran. Morning children."

Annie shrank back against Bridget, but Liam held his hand out to shake Carolyn's.

"You have lovely manners, young man," she said, smiling down at him. "Would you like some lemonade and cookies?"

"Yes please," Liam's eyes grew wide at the treat. "Come on Annie, get out quick before she changes her mind. Or Bridget says no."

The adults laughed. Annie let Liam lead her to the house, but she kept looking back at Bridget.

"Bridget, why don't you show the children where the kitchen is, and I can take the bag to your room?" Carolyn asked.

"We can do it together, Carolyn," Bridget answered.

The children were quiet as they walked around the house, their eyes staring at everything.

"Would you guys like to see your bedrooms? Once you have your cookie?" Carolyn asked.

Annie nodded and held up her new doll. "Can Sally Ann sleep in my bed too?"

"Of course, she can. Hello, Sally Ann, welcome to your new home," Carolyn greeted the doll as if she were real, earning a huge smile from Annie.

Bridget sighed with relief. This was going to be fine. She hung back as Carolyn showed the children their bedrooms.

"Is this all for me?" she heard Liam ask as he saw the room.

"Yes, son it is. We know you like to read,

hence the bookcases. We thought you might want to pick out some books to read. We will order you a desk as well. You can do your homework there after school," Geoff answered, his voice gruff with emotion.

"I don't have to get a job?" Liam asked.

"You will have chores to do to help your ma," Geoff told him.

Liam looked as if he couldn't believe what Geoff was saying.

"My bed is very big," Annie pointed out. "Is Bridget going to sleep there with me?"

"Yes Annie, when Bridget is here, she can share with you if you both like that. There is another room for Bridget though."

"You have more rooms than a hotel."

Liam's comment helped once more but feeling overwhelmed, Bridget stepped outside to get some air. It wasn't long before Brian followed her.

"You doing alright?" he asked.

"No. I mean yes. Oh, I don't know."

"You're doing the best you can for those

children. They won't want for anything. You know that."

"I know. And Carolyn has asked me to consider this my home when I come back to Riverside. But I can't help thinking my ma would be turning in her grave at my giving up the children."

"Bridget you didn't give up anything. You're helping everyone. Not just the children, but the Reeses too. Have you seen the looks on their faces? They're like kids at Christmas." Brian looked into the distance. "This ranch is a mighty fine home. Much better than any I could ever provide."

"Don't you dare put yourself down like that, Brian Curran. Some day you are going to have a wife and family and they will be lucky to have you."

"Yes, ma'am," he said, giving her a salute that made Bridget burst out laughing.

"Sorry, I did sound bossy, didn't I?"

"Yes, ma'am. Just like a big sister is supposed to sound. Those children are lucky to have you, Bridget."

They waited outside as the Reeses took some time to get to know the children and vice versa. Squeals of laughter told them things were working out just fine.

Bridget walked toward the horse corral, delighted to find a horse come forward. She stood stroking the mare's nose.

"When do you leave?" Brian asked.

"I think after a couple of days. I wrote to tell Father Nelson I'm coming back. He won't be happy," she said.

"I thought they wanted help with the trains," Brian said.

"They do, but he won't want me back in New York. Only, I have to check on Kathleen."

"And Maura?"

"Yes, her too. I don't agree with what she did but she's my sister and I can't walk away from her."

"Do you think you'll come back soon?" Brian asked.

"I don't think that would be wise. I will come back, but not for a while. The children need to settle and much as Carolyn and Geoff have made me welcome, I know they want their little family to bond. I would just get in the way."

"I will keep an eye on things for you, Bridget. Not that I think there will be anything wrong, but I can write and let you know how happy they are."

"Thank you, Brian, that would help a lot."

"You are a wonderful woman, Bridget Collins. I hope you find what you are looking for."

"I hope you do too, Brian. I really hope you do."

"This is where you two been hiding. Brian, I wondered if I might steal you away. Liam tells me you are very good with animals. I got a sick horse, can't tell what's wrong with her. Would you have a look?" Geoff asked Brian, Liam following right behind him.

"Sure. Excuse us Bridget."

Bridget watched as they walked away. She sensed a friendship was building there too.

AFTER LUNCH, Brian left to go back to his own farm. He promised to return the next day to check on the horse and see the children. Bridget went for a walk back into town to give the little family some space. The stagecoach was due to arrive that afternoon. Maybe she could send a couple of posts back with it. She would check with Mrs. Grayson. Geoff offered to lend her a horse, but she wanted to walk.

CHAPTER 52

arl Watson stepped down from the stagecoach. The town was even smaller than he'd imagined. Just what was he doing here? She was probably married by now. He would look like a fool, embarrassing both himself and her.

"Good afternoon, can I help you?"

Carl looked up to find a woman looking at him, her expression friendly but slightly wary.

"Thank you, kindly ma'am. I wondered if there might be a hotel I could book a room in?" Even as he spoke, he knew the answer. Who would build a hotel in a town with barely two streets?

"I have some rooms to rent," the woman said. "You from New York?"

Surprised, Carl nodded. The woman's friendly expression vanished.

"What did you say your name was?" she asked.

"My apologies, ma'am. My name's Carl Watson."

At that, her smile reappeared. He wondered if she was suffering from heat exposure. He looked around, but there didn't seem to be anyone else.

"Why didn't you say so, Mr. Watson? Come along in. I have freshly made lemonade in the kitchen. My husband, he does love a cool drink on a hot day like this."

Feeling as if perhaps he had sunstroke, Carl followed the peculiar woman into her home. Why was the woman speaking to him as if they were friends?

"Are you planning on staying long?" she asked him.

"No ma'am, a day or two at most. I just wanted to look up a..." What would he call Miss Collins? A friend? "Some children who were on the same train as me."

"The Collins children," she said, nodding. "Oh, what fine young 'uns they are. I miss them already."

"Miss them, ma'am?" Was he too late? They had moved on already?

"Yes, they moved out to their new home on the farm just this morning. You would think they had been gone a year already. Such a joy to have around. I would have adopted them myself if I was younger."

He had missed her by one day.

"When is the next stage, ma'am?" he asked, feeling defeated.

"Not till Wednesday. But you aren't in a hurry to leave, are you? You just got here."

"I think I may have been mistaken in coming. I don't wish to be a burden, perhaps you could show me the room. I assume cash will be acceptable."

"Now young man you sit there, and you listen to me. You just arrived, and you want to leave already? Didn't you come here to see someone?"

"Well yes, ma'am, but I don't think she, well, what I mean is, she's already..." he trailed off, not wanting to think about Bridget married and living with her new husband.

The woman tsked. "You came all this way to see her and you're running way before you do. What sort of man are you?"

Carl couldn't believe his ears. This stranger was chastising him like one would a child.

He stood up again.

"Ma'am I can't help feeling I'm in the wrong place. Perhaps I should just rent a gig to get me to the nearest big town."

"You came here to see Miss Collins, didn't you? Land sakes lad, but you aren't going to get her to marry you if you go running off in the wrong direction."

Carl sat down.

"You know about me?"

"I sure do. The children couldn't tell me enough about you. Bridget, I mean Miss Collins, she didn't say much but she didn't have to. She got the same look in her eyes you got when I mentioned her name. I don't know how you city folks behave, but around here you got to move quickly. There is only one woman for every nine or ten men so if you want Miss Collins, you need to move quickly."

"But she was to marry—"

"Brian Curran, a lovely man altogether but totally wrong for Miss Collins. He needs a wife who would be happy to live on his farm and raise a family. Bridget was born with a bigger purpose. Her heart is so full of love for those around her, she's got to go and help those children."

Carl struggled to follow along. "So, she didn't get married?"

"Do you need your ears washed out? Didn't you hear what I said? No, she didn't marry him. She is a free as a bird. I am so happy you're here. I mean, I wasn't sure when I saw you all dandied up standing on the street. I thought you might be that horrible Mr. Oaks. That's why I wasn't so pleasant. But then you told me your name and I knew why you were here."

Mr. Oaks? Was that the name of the man Bridget was running from? Before he could clarify, a bell signaled someone was in the store.

"Well don't you know it. Mr. Grayson has gone missing again. Why that man thinks I can handle everything is beyond me. Excuse me while I go find out what they want. You don't go running off, you hear?"

Bemused, Carl stayed where he was. He couldn't blame the elusive Mr. Grayson for disappearing. His wife talked a lot.

He sat waiting, trying to figure out what Mrs. Grayson had said. Had Bridget really not gotten married?

"Mr. Watson, what are you doing here?"

He stood up so fast the chair fell over behind him. His coffee went flying across the table.

"Now don't you go messing up my kitchen," Mrs. Grayson wandered back in from the shop and pretended to scold him. "Why don't you take him out for a walk, Bridget. He seems rather strange so don't wander far."

He was strange? Talk about the pot calling the kettle black. Bridget looked paler than he remembered, the black shadows under her eyes lending her an air of frailty.

"Miss Collins, forgive my coming unannounced, but I just had to see you. I mean I had to check on you and the children. It's my duty you see as—"

"Will you just tell her the truth. You came to see her. Not the children, just her," Mrs. Grayson blurted out.

He was about to argue but Bridget's voice stopped him.

"You did?" she asked.

He couldn't miss the hope in her tone or in

her eyes. He clamped down on the urge to do a little dance on the street. Scamp was already being too active for both of them, running around with his tail wagging behind him.

"Yes, I did. I know it was wrong of me, but I hope you forgive me." Please do more than that. Tell me I was right to come.

"I do, it's just, well…it's such a surprise. Oh, I don't know what to say," Bridget said.

"Say yes when he asks you to marry him, which he should have done by now," Mrs. Grayson said. "Do New Yorkers always take this long to do anything? It's a wonder any-thing gets done back east."

"Mrs. Grayson," their voices called out in unison. The older lady turned slightly pink.

"I should go check on Mr. Grayson. I won't be but a moment. I can leave you alone, but the door will be open."

Carl didn't know where to look, he was so embarrassed. Judging by Bridget's pink cheeks, so was she.

"Miss Collins, Bridget, please have a seat."

She sat and looked at him expectantly.

"Mrs. Grayson says you didn't get married. I don't need to know the reasons why, but I can't help but hope it may be because you had a change of heart."

He waited for her to say something, but she didn't.

"I didn't want to speak before as it wasn't seemly but well, the thing is, I have grown very fond of you."

"Fond?" She sounded amused.

He glanced up, but she had an innocent expression on her face. Darn it anyway, but he didn't know what to say.

"Yes, one might say I fell…"

"He fell in love with you. You fell in love with him. Now can you hurry up? I need to put the meat in the oven. At this rate, Mr. Grayson will think he is back on starvation rations during the war."

Mrs. Grayson's voice carried through from the store. Amused, they exchanged a look, but Bridget didn't move toward him. Using his finger, he tried to pull his collar loose, it was difficult to breathe.

"I've waited years to find someone like you, Miss Collins. A woman who knows how to love with all her heart, whose love for these children knows no bounds, a woman I admire…"

"Admire?" she interrupted, frowning slightly.

"I mean respect. I respect you," he mumbled. This wasn't easy. He saw by the way she was looking at him he was making rather a mess of things. Oh, how he wished he had studied the works of Bronte and Shakespeare rather than the theology books he had learned by rote.

He stepped closer, taking her hand.

"Miss Collins, Bridget, I…you showed me how to find happiness. How to open my heart and trust my feelings. I...I love you. Will you marry me Miss Collins?"

"Yes."

. . .

MRS. GRAYSON POPPED her head around the door. "Is it safe to come in yet?"

"Leave the poor young 'uns be and make me a cup of coffee," Mr. Grayson said. "There's a good wife."

"Shall we take that walk?" Carl asked Bridget who nodded.

"Don't be long. I will include both of you for lunch," Mrs. Grayson called over to them.

"Son, do yourself a favor and show our Bridget you wear the trousers from the start. Otherwise your wife will be too big for her britches, just like mine," Mr. Grayson said with a wink.

Carl almost pushed Bridget out the door in his haste to get away.

CHAPTER 53

ridget couldn't believe her eyes, he was here. In Riverside Springs. And he'd asked her to marry him.

"I thought you had to go and check on the children," she said.

"I did. I saw some of them. Lizzie and Jacob both send you their love. They are as happy as could be with their wonderful new family."

"I'm so glad," she said, feeling relieved. "All the children were precious, but I admit Jacob won a special space in my heart."

"He's partly the reason I'm here," he said.

She waited for him to explain.

"He asked me why I had let you go. He told me off quite severely. In fact, he called me a chicken."

Bridget covered her mouth in an attempt to trap the laughter from escaping.

"I know you want to laugh but it wasn't funny at the time. I was quite insulted." He stopped walking and turned to take her in his arms. "Bridget, I was such a fool to risk letting you go."

"You didn't have much of a choice. You're an honorable man and I was promised to another." She didn't add that she had wished several times he wasn't so honorable. That was one thing nobody need ever know.

"I still should have made my feelings clear. But I wasn't able to provide you with financial security. I don't earn a lot as a part time teacher being away so much with the trains, but I can look for a proper position. When I think how close I came to losing you..."

"But you didn't," she reassured him. "Brian, he's the man I was going to marry, he and I were never suited. He is a kind, considerate man, and a good friend now. But my heart was always yours."

She moved closer to him. He cupped her face in his hands and brought his lips slowly down to meet hers. It was the most fleeting of kisses, yet it held so much promise.

"Mrs. Grayson thought I was that bounder Oaks. She was very protective of you. Why didn't you tell me the whole story before?" he asked.

"How could I? It was bad enough you knew I was planning on marrying a stranger. But to also admit I was running from a man I stabbed would be far too embarrassing."

"You should have stabbed him harder. I can't believe he got away with it," Carl said, looking angry.

"The rich will always get away with things. It is just the way of the world. But let's stop talking about him. I need to ask you something, Carl."

"Anything," he said.

"I would like to work with you," Bridget said. "For a while, at least. I want to help find homes for children like Annie, Liam, Sally, Lizzie, and Jacob. To find them proper families."

"Are you serious?"

"Yes. Why? Do you not agree with married women working?"

"No, my darling, I never believed it possible I would find a wonderful woman who not only would share my life but my goal as well. I believe our role is to help as many children as we can. Together we can change lives."

"I hope so, Carl."

"Do you want Liam and Annie to travel with us?"

"No, I agreed to their being adopted."

His raised eyebrow prompted her to tell him the whole story about meeting the Reeses on the train.

"Annie and Liam love them already, so they will be very happy here in Riverside Springs. I like this community a lot."

"Oh?"

"I would like to bring Kathleen, and Maura if she will come, out here to Riverside Springs. I have to ask Lily to find a wife for Brian. I promised him I would. Maybe in time, we could have our home here too." Bridget turned to look around at the small town that had captured her heart. "Can you imagine how many of the ladies from the sanctuary could find new lives out here? Not necessarily in this town, not until it grows at least, but in this state. It could be a chance to start over."

"Something tells me that life with you will never be boring," he said.

"Is that a yes?" she asked, her heart thumping madly as she waited for him to answer. He would agree, wouldn't he? If he said no, she would have to choose between a life with him or helping the children. The seconds seemed to tick by slower than ever. She glanced up and he was staring at her.

"Carl?" she prompted.

"How could I say no?"

Bridget smiled as he took her in his arms and swung her around in a circle before pulling her closer to steal another kiss.

"Let's go find Reverend Franklin and see if he can marry us before we head back to New York," Carl said. "I don't want to spend another moment in your company as single man."

EPILOGUE

*A*s it turned out, Carl had to wait a few days to marry his bride. Reverend Franklin insisted on giving Bridget time to adjust to the change in her circumstances. He didn't think it appropriate for her to get married a day after placing her siblings up for adoption. So, Carl stayed with Brian Curran during that time as it wasn't appropriate for him to stay in the same place as his bride. Bridget wanted to stay in town with Mrs. Grayson to give the Reeses time to come together as a family. She also wanted to see how much interest she could generate for Kathleen's new venture.

The wedding took place on the Sunday after Carl arrived in Riverside Springs. Bridget wore a dress she had sewn herself from fabric given to her by Carolyn Rees. She and Carolyn made a dress for Annie who looked pretty as a picture. Liam walked Bridget up the aisle, a look of pride on his face although he kept looking to his new Pa as if to check he was doing things the right way.

At the party afterwards, Carl couldn't bear to let Bridget out of his sight but her new friends had different ideas. They all gathered for a meal at the Reeses' ranch.

"Do you believe your sister will want to travel out here, Bridget?" Shannon Williams asked.

"Kathleen will, she is very much a family person. Maura, she's a different case. She mentioned joining a religious order once, but I suspect she was speaking from grief. Not that there is anything wrong with having a calling,"

Bridget corrected herself as Reverend Franklin shot her a look of mock incredulity.

Carl looked around the small gathering. What an example this town could provide to other areas. The residents were working together to see what, if anything, Riverdale Springs could do to help the orphans from New York.

"I hope they both decide to come out as I shall miss you, Bridget. We all will. Carl, you must bring her to see us soon," Shannon said.

"I'm not sure I have much choice in the matter," Carl answered. "My wife is very strong-willed."

Bridget flushed as he looked at her, still not quite believing his luck. Her agreement to marry him had led to him opening up to her about his past. She had encouraged him to talk to Brian, Mitch, and Shannon about their experiences, feeling it was better he know that some adults didn't regret being placed on the orphan trains.

"Actually, I was wondering if someone

would volunteer to vet the families here for us, should any of them decide they wanted to take in a child." Carl asked. "We need people in each city to try to ensure only those who will treat the children kindly are approved."

"That's a job for Mrs. Grayson," Shannon said. "She knows everything about everyone."

"I heard that," Mrs. Grayson replied.

"I meant you to. You know we all love you despite your eccentric ways."

"Me? I'm as normal as they come aren't I, Carl?"

Carl pretended not to hear her. While he liked her more and understood her need to protect Bridget, he still hadn't quite gotten over their first encounter. Still, no better woman could be appointed to look after the children's interests.

"If we had more women come out, then we might get more people looking to foster children. I know single men like Brian wouldn't come forward. I am guessing the Society would prefer married couples to adopt," Shannon added.

"Well, it seems my wife has some ideas on that front too," Carl said. "Tell them, Bridget."

He thought her plan was an excellent one but wasn't sure if everyone would agree.

"When I ran away from my attacker, Mr. Oaks, I fled to a place called Carmel's Mission. Lily Doherty set up this sanctuary as a safe place for those women and children who desperately needed help. There are so many who need Lily's help, but she can only house a certain amount. I thought, given the shortage of women out here in towns just like Riverside Springs, we could encourage the ladies to leave New York behind and make a fresh start here."

"That's a wonderful idea," Shannon said, her eyes lit up with excitement.

"Who will pay their train fares?" Mrs. Grayson, ever practical, asked.

"Lily has some wealthy contacts. She will be able to help with that and some of the ladies will have some savings. If the single men of the town were willing to marry, then perhaps they could chip in for the rail fare."

"Bridget Collins—I mean Watson, you never cease to amaze me with your wonderful ideas. So, when will you put your plans into place?" Mrs Grayson asked.

"Carl and I wish to visit the children we placed during our trip out here. Then we will return to New York. It will take some time, but I imagine we would return in approximately six months' time."

Carl nodded his head in agreement. He was excited to see what they would be able to achieve working together. One thing he was certain of, no child they met would ever be placed in a home like that endured by Mitch or himself.

"Bridget, Mitch would like to ask you and Carl a favor. Go on darling, ask."

"I hope this isn't an inconvenience, Bridget, but I wondered if you might be able to check the records in New York to see if you could find my sister. Annie was only three when we were put on the train. I have written but nobody seems to know what happened to her."

"I will do what I can, Mitch," Bridget assured him. "If you could write out the details you remember, I will certainly try."

"Thank you, Bridget. And you too, Carl." Mitch raised his glass "To fresh starts and new friendships."

Everyone raised their glass knowing this was only the beginning.

* * *

TO ALL MY WONDERFUL READERS, I hope you enjoyed this book as much as I loved writing it. It made me cry as well but I feel the stories of these children need to be made public. It was a sad time in history and not just confined to the USA. The stories of how orphans were treated in my own country, Ireland are horrifying, all the more so as they continued until the 1970's and in some cases the 1980's. I have now completed book two of this series. In book two, we find out what happened to Bridget's brothers and also we learn more about Bella and her adventures. I have included a sneak peak.

Orphan Train Trials

CHAPTER *One*

Kathleen Collins read the letter from her sister Bridget quickly, greedily consuming all her news.

"Has Bridget listened to our advice to stay away from New York?"

Kathleen looked up at Lily's question. She hated upsetting this kind woman who had done so much to help her family. She shook her head. "She says they will be here in about two weeks. First, they are going to visit Doctor Powell and his wife, the people who adopted Sally."

"I wonder if they were able to help Sally's limp. She was such a lovely happy child with her beautiful smile." Lily sighed causing Kathleen to look up in concern.

"Kathleen, I admit to being torn. I am looking forward to seeing your sister again and congratulating her on her marriage, but I don't want to place her in danger."

"Lily, it's been almost a year since we left the factory. Surely, Mr. Oaks will have forgotten about Bridget now. He should have other things on his mind with the financial crash."

Lily smiled sadly. "You would think so, especially with over sixteen thousand businesses folding. Charlie said one in six men are now out of work. But, somehow, Mr. Oaks and his ilk tend to survive, perhaps thrive in difficult times like these. I heard from Inspector Pascal Griffin. Oaks is a man who never forgets, especially someone like Bridget."

Kathleen exchanged a glance with her friend, Bella. They knew how difficult life was in New York with the increased unemployment meaning more visitors to the sanctuary. Still, she hoped Inspector Griffin was wrong, although he wouldn't have got to such a senior level in the police force if he wasn't usually correct in these matters.

She was dying to see Bridget, she missed her and Annie and Liam. She also wanted to get to know her new brother-in-law better. Having only met him briefly when Annie and Liam joined the orphan train, she couldn't help but wonder what her vivacious older sister saw in such a stern, sad man. Yet Bridget was happy, more than happy. Her letters flowed with joy over her new role as an outplacement agent. Even when she wrote of the things that annoyed her, her tone was one of someone who believed in the work they were doing. She continually praised her husband Carl.

"Bridget won't be staying in New York for long, so she should be fine," Lily said, bending to reach the knitting by her chair. They were in her private sitting room taking advantage of some quiet time. Charlie was away with work and Lily had to wait for Mini Mike or Tommy to collect her to escort her home. Charlie had left strict instructions on the care his wife was to receive. Lily joked Charlie must think she was the first woman to have a child, but everyone knew he was just being careful. They had been married a long time, almost five years.

"How is Inspector Griffin?" Kathleen asked in a bid to change the conversation away from Oaks and danger. "The papers are full of stories about how the New York police department needs to be cleaned up."

"I think there are more criminals in the force than outside it," Bella said, not looking up from the sketch she was working on. Kathleen looked over her shoulder, trying to see the dress. Bella had a wonderful eye for detail. They used to take walks down to Fifth Avenue to view the dresses in the store windows. When they got back, Bella would take out her sketch pad and draw similar designs to those she had seen in the stores. She really was very clever.

"Bella, that's not true," Lily reprimanded gently.

Bella put her pencil down and looked Lily straight in the face. "Yes, it is, Lily. Every woman who comes here has a similar story about paying the police bribes, either in cash or favors." Bella's face turned various shades of pink, partly from anger at the injustices the women faced, and partly from embarrassment Kathleen surmised.

"Those men are supposed to protect every-one, but they don't care about the children in the tenements. They just lock them up."

"Bella, I know you are upset about young Dillon and Sammy being arrested, but they were caught in the act," Kathleen said gently. "You can't blame the police for picking them up."

"Can't I? Those kids had to do it, the gangs told them to. What would happen to them if they refused? The police are afraid of the East-mans and the Five Pointers."

The gangs ruled New York, that much was true, although there were police officers trying to fight back. But corruption was rife, and many law enforcers looked the other way depending on which gang was involved. There were rumors the government was going to do something to sort out the corruption but, as yet, nothing much had happened. But there were still some police who wore their uniform with pride and served their community as best they could.

"Bella, that's unfair. Inspector Griffin was talking about that very thing when he called to check on us over the weekend. He said there are moves being made to get the gang situation under control but, in the meantime, we have to be patient," Lily said, her tired tone making Kathleen wish Mini Mike or Tommy would come back to take Lily home.

"I'm sorry, Lily." Bella looked contrite, "I just can't bear the sight of those kids in the cells. I know they act all tough but putting children in with real criminals is just wrong." Bella pursed her lips together as she screwed her eyes shut. Not one tear escaped but Kathleen had seen her friend's eyes fill up. She squeezed her arm gently trying to show her she cared.

"Bella, you reminded me. I can't believe I forgot," Lily said, sitting straighter in the chair. "Being pregnant is making me forgetful. Father Nelson spoke to me yesterday about a group of orphaned children coming to us from a prison somewhere north of here," Lily explained.

"A prison?" Kathleen clarified.

"Yes. It is bad enough when youngsters like Sammy or Dillon get picked up and thrown in a cell for a night. But these children have been living in the prison. Their only crime is that of being poor and orphaned. The local authorities maintain it's because the orphanages are overflowing."

"You don't believe them?" Kathleen asked.

Lily picked up the teapot and poured more

tea into their cups. Lily sat back farther in her seat as if taking time to compose her thoughts.

"I believe the existing facilities are over-crowded, but that is not where the blame lies. Until our government views the needs of vulnerable children with the same importance as other issues, there will never be enough money or safe places for the people who need them most." Lily stopped talking, an apologetic look on her face. "Forgive me, girls. Charlie tells me not to get on my soap box."

"Nothing to apologize for," Kathleen said. "I wish there were more people who think like you do, Lily. I feel so bad for those we left behind in the tenements. When Mam was alive, she used to share what we had with the families who lived around us. Like Mrs. Fleming does."

"Speaking of Mrs. Fleming, would you like to come and visit her with me?" Lily asked. "I am going tomorrow night—Mini Mike and Tommy will be with us. I had a message to call on her last week but as I had a chill, Charlie ordered me to bed."

"Yes, please. I would love to see her," Kathleen answered. "Bella, would you like to come with us. Mrs. Fleming is such a lovely lady. Her husband, Dave, and children are nice too. They were very good to us when my mam died." Kathleen had been thrilled Bella had opened up so much and become a close friend. She would never replace Bridget in her affections, but she had helped her through a very lonely time. She wanted Bella to meet Mrs. Fleming who did so much work in the community helping families to help themselves.

Bella looked up from her sketching, "Yes, please."

"That's settled then," Lily said, smiling at Bella. Kathleen knew Lily wanted to get Bella to be more trusting of people. To see that not everyone was as horrible as the people who had mistreated her when she was younger.

"Kathleen, can you ask Cook to bake a few more batches of cookies? They always disappear quickly. We'll need some blankets and some clothes as well. You know the drill by now," Lily said, smiling at Kathleen, making her feel warm inside. Since Bridget had left, Kathleen had gone out with Lily on her rounds visiting those families who couldn't, or wouldn't, come to the sanctuary. She couldn't say she enjoyed going back to the tenements. She didn't. There was no comparison between her current home and the overcrowded, wretched squalor she had once lived. She was so grateful Lily had taken her family in.

"I'll go now and get organized. Thank you, Lily." She stood and gathered the cups to take the tray with her. Bella stood to answer the door, they all recognized Tommy's knock.

"Evening, ladies." Tommy acknowledged them. "Are you ready to go home, Miss Lily?"

"Yes, thank you, Tommy." Lily beamed at her friend and protector. "Wait, Kathleen, what about Maura? Would she like to come with us?"

Kathleen didn't look at Lily but stared at a

point above her head. Embarrassed at her sister's behavior, she wasn't sure if Lily knew of the latest problems Maura had caused. Bella didn't make any comment. Kathleen thought it was loyal of her not to complain to Lily about how badly Maura had treated her over the last month in particular.

"Why don't you ask Maura?" Lily asked when Kathleen didn't respond. "She may find it good to get out of the sanctuary and back into the real world if only for a few hours."

Kathleen wasn't at all sure Maura would say yes, so she just kept quiet.

BUY ORPHAN TRAIN Trials to keep reading.

HISTORICAL NOTE

Historical Note:

Although my story is fictional, and the characters are only alive in my imagination, Charles Brace was a real person. His idea to help the poor of New York, in particular the "orphans" (many were not real orphans, having one or both parents still alive in some cases), was to send them by train for placement in families across the United States. The scheme was supposed to organize what we would now call foster care rather than adoptions. But many children were adopted if often informally.

He had the best of intentions, of that there is no doubt. At that time, children were routinely housed in asylums. Brace believed that more care was given to the costs of looking after the children and the upkeep of the properties than to any individual child.

For some, being sent on these trains was the start of a brand new happy life. For others, it was the start of a period of abject cruelty. For the majority, it was something in between. Many people took advantage of the system to employ what we would call today, child labor.

The rules of the scheme were clear and written to protect both those who fostered and the children. The children were supposed to be guaranteed good treatment, with schooling, meals, clothing, and shelter. The reality was that the sheer scale of the country, together with poor transport links, meant there were not sufficient resources available to check these rules were being adhered to. Where placing agents were able to check on children, those being mistreated often lied about their circumstances for fear of yet another beating or additional punishment.

Many of the children suffered abuse but given the Victorian standards of the day, not much is known about the numbers of potential victims. There was some acknowledgement of the abuse young girls could be subjected to but that endured by young boys was almost universally ignored. If a claim of abuse was made, more often than not the child would not be believed. This was particularly the case if the foster parent was wealthy. People of that time believed abuse only happened in poorer homes!

The first train left New York in 1854 and these trains continued until the early 1930s. It is impossible to know for sure how many children travelled the rails, but estimates are circa 200,000 children were placed in new homes. Several thousand adults also used a similar scheme to find new places to live.

In my story, I do not distinguish between Catholic and Protestant faiths for the purpose of the book. But in reality, the Catholic Church via the New York Foundling Hospital began sending their own version of the orphan trains called the Mercy Trains in the late 1860s. The Foundling Hospital had slightly different criteria. All the children who traveled on a Mercy train had been placed with Mid-West Families before the child left New York. So, these children were spared the often-cruel rejections standing up in front of a town waiting to be picked would cause.

Did the scheme work? Not always, as our fictional character Bella and those of Mitch and Brian illustrated. But there were also those like Sally, Jacob, and Lizzie who were adopted by wonderful people and given new opportunities.

Brace did not believe in sibling attachment with the result that more often than not, the Outplacement Society made few efforts to keep families intact. There are many stories of siblings being separated never to be reunited again. Sometimes the children were kept in orphanages in New York until they grew older and therefore more desirable in the eyes of the prospective foster parents. It appears the majority of these orphanages were quite humane places and not like those outlined in Charles Dicken's novels.

Other cities followed the example of New York. In Boston, three different organizations being the Children's Mission, the New England Home for Little Wanderers and the Home for Destitute Catholic Children also sent children by train to the mid-west.

It is not unusual for different countries to use various methods of solving what they consider a poverty crisis. In more recent times, we have seen much media coverage of the controversial decision by the British Government to send many British "orphans" to settle in Australia at the end of the Second World War.

Would the lives of these children have been better if Brace had never come up with the placing out scheme and they had been left behind to live on the streets of New York? For the majority, the answer would be no. It is all too easy to look back and judge the orphan trains by the standards of today. But in the 1850s and beyond, the children convicted of petty crimes were sent to prison with adults. Children could be tried and hanged for murder and other crimes. The lives of the poor were worse than anything we could imagine. Immigration meant New York couldn't cope with the numbers of people arriving every day. The melting point of different nationalities, races, religious beliefs etc. led to rising tensions and high unemployment. At a time when there were no social welfare payments, Brace knew something had to be done and he tried his best in spite of opposition from almost every side. The religious institutions didn't want "their" orphans going to places where they might come in contact with "less worthy" religions. The majority of the rich believed the poor brought about their own misery by living in filth and squalor.

If you would like to read more about the

real life "orphan trains" a couple of books I would recommend include:

The Orphan Trains – Placing Out in America by Marilyn Irvin Holt.

Orphan Trains – The story of Charles Loring Brace and the Children He saved and Failed by Stephen O'Connor.

Orphan Trains to Missouri by Michael D Patrick and Evelyn Goodrich Trickel.